Eli's Songs

ELI'S SONGS
by Monte Killingsworth

Margaret K. McElderry Books
New York

Maxwell Macmillan Canada
Toronto

Maxwell Macmillan International
New York   Oxford   Singapore   Sydney

Margaret K. McElderry Books
Macmillan Publishing Company
866 Third Avenue
New York, NY 10022

Maxwell Macmillan Canada, Inc.
1200 Eglinton Avenue East
Suite 200
Don Mills, Ontario M3C 3N1
Macmillan Publishing Company is part of the Maxwell Communication
Group of Companies.

First edition
Printed in the United States of America
10   9   8   7   6   5   4   3   2   1

Library of Congress Cataloging-in-Publication Data
Killingsworth, Monte.
Eli's songs / by Monte Killingsworth.
p.   cm.
Summary: Shipped off to relatives in Oregon while his father is
touring with his rock band, twelve-year-old Eli comes to love the
magnificent trees of a nearby forest and tries to prevent their
imminent destruction.
ISBN 0-689-50527-2
[1. Conservation of natural resources—Fiction.   2. Oregon—
Fiction.]   I. Title.
PZ7.K5575E1   1991
[Fic]—dc20   91-6452

for DEBORAH
who knows about trees

1

Leave the crowded city
You got nothing to do
Ain't it just a pity
They're just picking on you

Born in California
Now you're leaving it behind
Head out to the country
You know it's so unkind

Elixir James Connolly was still trying to talk his way out of being exiled to Oregon when the red convertible Cadillac with Rick at the wheel burbled into the Valencia Drive Greyhound station and stopped near the front doors, in a tow-away zone.

It was a muggy June day in Los Angeles. Dust clung to the palm trees. Smog hid the hills. Far away a siren screamed and then died away.

1

"Hey, Rick," he tried, "what about our camping trips and that raft we were going to get and all that other stuff we talked about. Remember that? Remember when you said if I passed social studies . . ."

It was no use. Rick wasn't listening. He was pulling Eli's luggage, stereo, guitar, and amplifier out of the trunk and stacking them on the sidewalk. Rick had heard it all before and he had an answer for everything.

Rick was the lead singer and guitarist for Styletto, a rhythm-and-blues band that was really going places and he had more important things on his mind now than camping trips.

"Hey, Eli, what's all the junk in this box?"

Eli is what everyone called Elixir. Everyone but his mother, whom he hadn't seen in years. She was the one who had decided on the name in the first place. Eli remembered her always talking about the Elixir, and how he was supposed to make the world a good place again. She was pretty strange, he guessed, the way she carried on like that. When he had been a little kid he had mostly wished his name was Fred or Jim or something besides Elixir, but now that he was almost thirteen—well, in seven months—and a songwriter, he figured a name that was a little different helped him stand out from the crowd, made him unique. But Eli was as far as he went; nobody called him Elixir.

"What is all this stuff, Eli?" Rick, halfway into the trunk of the big Cadillac, balancing on one alligator-booted foot, looked pretty comical.

2

"What stuff, Rick?" Though Rick was Eli's father, Eli never called him Dad. Rick was Rick. Eli was trying not to laugh as he watched his soon-to-be-famous-rock-star father practically lying in the trunk of his flashy red convertible, picking up something that had spilled out of a cardboard box. "Oh, that stuff."

Rick had discovered Eli's writing box. "Eli, you know I told you that you can't take our entire apartment to Oregon with you. Look at this. Fifty-dozen legal pads, and these pens. How many colors of marker does it take to write a song, anyway? Tape, paper clips . . . Holy Toledo, Eli, don't you think they have stuff like this in Oregon? Like maybe they still plow the fields with oxen and write with feathers? And did you really think they were just going to throw this box on the bus like this, no top, no nothing, like maybe the driver had a special place reserved just for your junk?"

Eli knew better than to try to argue when Rick got like this.

"Okay, okay, Rick. Probably I can find blackened sticks from campfires and write on cliffs. Maybe they still do use those feathers. Except I think they call them quills. Hey, I'll think of something."

Rick had finished putting back Eli's writing stuff into the box and slammed the trunk shut, leaving the box inside. He was gathering up suitcases and the amplifier, leaving the guitar and the Anvil case of electronic goodies for Eli.

"You know," Rick said, "rock songs are supposed to

3

be simple and direct, the more straight-ahead, the better. The people listening can't tell what color the ink was when the song was written. It might be good for you to try writing with just a pencil and a piece of paper. I'm real sure they have those up in Oregon. Remember: the simpler, the better." With that, Rick flipped his hair back over his shoulders and, balancing Eli's belongings under both arms, headed for the big glass doors of the bus station.

Eli did not want to go to Oregon for the summer. He did not want to leave Los Angeles for the summer. He kidded around with Rick partly because it was his nature to keep his feelings to himself and partly because he knew Rick felt guilty about sending him away and Eli didn't want to make things worse and possibly get in the way of Rick's success. But while he was good old easy-come-easy-go Eli on the outside, on the inside things were very different.

For one thing, Eli felt ashamed that his father thought he had to be "watched," like he was a little kid. True, he had never had to fend for himself for more than a few days at a time. But he was sure that he could survive the summer somehow. He had lots of friends, didn't he? And they had parents, right? And what about Mr. Williams in the apartment next door? Eli spent a lot of time over there with that old guy and hadn't he offered to take care of Eli for the summer while Rick was gone?

Or what about Eli's best idea, going along on the tour with Rick and Styletto. What a trip that would be!

But Rick had nixed all of these plans. Especially the last one. Eli wasn't sure what exactly went on during a major concert tour, although he thought he could guess, but whatever it was, Rick made it clear—crystal clear—that Eli was not going to be a part of it. "You have lots of time before you're ready for that," he had said. Like to a little kid.

That hurt.

Eli had been to many Styletto concerts and dances, sometimes on the road for three or four days in a row. He had sort of considered himself a member of the band. At least they all liked him. Once in a while, they even performed one of his songs, making a big deal of the fact that it was written by the lead singer's twelve-year-old son.

Eli's hair was almost as long as his father's, although it was blond and straight like his mother's hair, rather than dark and curly, and he wore a diamond earring that was a match for the one in Rick's left ear. He played a pretty mean Stratocaster and was getting real handy—that's the way Phil the bass player put it—at setting up the sound system for a Styletto performance.

Just like part of the band.

So when their second single climbed even higher than the first and hovered in the teens for over a month, and when Rick's band that had worked so hard for so long was invited to open shows all over the U.S. in big stadiums and concert halls, no one in Styletto was happier than Eli.

But a whole summer on the road just wasn't in the cards, Eli guessed. Not for him.

Instead, he was being sent to Oregon to stay with Rick's brother Danny and his wife, Maud.

Oregon!

Eli had thought of little else since that night almost three weeks ago when Rick had told him the plan. He was thinking about it now, as he stood in the crowded station and waited for Rick to return from the counter where he was checking in the luggage—and doing whatever else you do, thought Eli, to make sure your kid gets on the right bus.

He looked around him. The bus station was like all bus stations: dirty tile, metal and brown plastic furniture, most of it torn, smelling of cigarettes and urine. Years of grime and filth left by millions of travelers. The palm trees outside the glass doors though, the bright sunshine, the fast cars and motorcycles cruising past on Valencia Drive, the girls in shorts giggling and pretending not to look at him—these things were pure Los Angeles to Eli. Things he liked. Things he didn't expect to find in Oregon.

Eli was still trying to take in the sights and sounds of L.A. when Rick returned. He had a little red, white, and blue folder.

"This is your ticket and your baggage claim. Bus

number one-seventeen. Leaves in ten minutes. You can carry on your guitar and the Anvil. You better get on now if you want to find a seat by the window."

Rick stopped talking. Eli guessed he was about as nervous and uncomfortable as he felt himself. They both stood with their hands in the front pockets of their jeans, not knowing quite what to say. Eli thought Rick looked pretty much like an overgrown boy and felt a wave of sympathy sweep over him, a warm wave. Someone's got to do something, he thought, and he found himself doing what he hadn't done for years. Eli threw both arms around his father and held on.

Sitting on the bus, cruising up the interstate, Eli couldn't remember exactly what had happened between that bear hug and the moment when he had watched Rick's Cadillac pull slowly onto Valencia Drive and disappear into traffic. He did remember the tears in his father's eyes though.

And as he watched the traffic slowly, silently, floating past the bus, he remembered something else. Never during the last three weeks, including the emotional farewell in the station, had Rick said when he would be returning to Los Angeles. Exactly when. He had always talked about the summer, but no precise date for his return had ever been mentioned.

Eli watched the brown fields of California disappear slowly into the night, and it occurred to him that he had no idea when he would be coming home.

2

The end of a long journey
Is really just the start
When you get through with all your traveling
You'll find you ain't so smart

There are some that try to help you
And some that put you down
But those people never let you forget
You just got into town

Fences. That was the first thing Eli noticed about Oregon. Fences everywhere. The road to Moffett was no exception. As soon as the Greyhound had turned right from the freeway exit there had been miles of rangeland stretching away from both sides of the straight, two-lane country road and, yes, fences holding it back. It wasn't clear whether the fences in Oregon were intended to keep something out or something in. Eli figured maybe both.

*   *   *

Moffett, Oregon, was a small town in the middle of the Willamette Valley. The bus went miles to get to it, through fields of cattle grazing, through forests, and across creeks and rivers. Then, just when Eli felt they might be lost, well, there it was. They came around a bend in the road and found the town, perched upon the highway as if it grew there. Neat little white houses nestled among huge poplar and fir trees. There were vegetable gardens in every yard. Fences.

Main Street was hot and treeless, lined with a hardware store, two taverns, a video store, a Rexall drugstore, and almost everything else the people of the small Oregon farm town would need.

Down each cross street Eli could see the trees and yards begin right behind the buildings on the main street. Unlike Los Angeles, where the stores and restaurants go for miles in every direction, all mixed in with the homes, business in Moffett was on this street only. Or so it seemed from the bus window.

The Greyhound station was at the far end of Main Street, just before the street turned back into a two-lane country road and curved out of town. When the bus hissed to a stop in the alley next to the squat little building, Eli was waiting at the door with his guitar in one hand and the Anvil case in the other. He was the only one getting off in Moffett. The driver took the baggage claim ticket and jumped off the bus with it. He slid open the big doors to the compartment under the bus, quickly loaded Eli's luggage and amp onto a hand-truck, which hung inside the compartment, and wheeled it toward the door of the station.

"You can just leave it out here if you want," said Eli. "And thanks for the ride," he said, even though the driver had only been driving the bus since Roseburg.

"Yeah, you bet." The fat driver grinned. He wasn't used to being appreciated. "Good luck, kid."

Eli watched the bus ease down the alley, then waited while it circled behind the station, came out on the next street down, then pulled onto Main Street again and headed back the same way it had come, toward the freeway. The driver raised a quick hand in salute and Eli nodded his head with a little grin, like he'd seen Rick do—Rick, whose hands always seemed to be full of amps and guitars. Eli stood where he had stepped off the bus, unsure of what to do next.

There were no cars in front of the small station. Eli gazed up and down the street. This was really hard to believe. It was late morning, probably about eleven o'clock—Eli didn't have a watch so he had to guess—and not one car was moving on the street. Not one! He had never seen a street with no cars on it except in those sci-fi films about the end of the world. Eli wondered if it was always this quiet here.

He put down his guitar and the case and went into the bus station. The man behind the counter in the back had on a Greyhound uniform and a cap. He was staring at Eli as though he might have just landed in a space-ship.

"I'm supposed to be meeting my aunt and uncle here," began Eli. "Danny and Maud."

The man in the uniform just continued to stare for a moment. Eli saw him glance nervously at the phone once or twice. Finally he said, "I don't know nothing about your aunt and uncle, boy." Then, after a pause, "This ain't no place just to be meeting people anyhow. This is a bus station. Greyhound business only. See the sign?"

Eli followed the man's eyes to a NO LOITERING sign. It took him a second to catch on.

"Hey, dude," Eli said in his best Los Angeles rock star voice, "I rode in here on one of your Hounds. This is official Greyhound business."

The skinny clerk took in Eli's hair and then the diamond stud in his left ear.

"Yeah, then where's your luggage?"

"Right outside. Where I had the driver leave it for me." Rock star voice. Eli rocked back on his bootheels, slid his hands into his pockets. "Guess I'll go out and wait with it. You know, my man," pause, one, two, three, "I do believe you have an attitude problem." He turned before the clerk could see the grin begin and sauntered, real slow, back out into the morning. Eli hoped that all the people in Moffett weren't this unfriendly and suspicious.

11

Eli didn't have to wait long. He had only begun to take in the sights and smells of Moffett when an old International pickup pulled into the parking space right in front of him and his uncle Danny got out and grabbed him in a huge bear hug right there on the sidewalk. Eli and Danny began talking, both at once, and started grabbing things from the stack on the sidewalk.

Rick and his younger brother Danny were opposites in almost every way, but Eli thought there were at least two things that showed the difference between them most clearly. First and most obvious was their hair. Rick had the classic rock star look. His hair was long and shaggy, coming nearly halfway down his back, and it was full and curly, so that it moved with every step he took. Rick kept his dark beard trimmed real close to his face and took care to have every hair in place.

Danny looked, well, just the opposite. His hair was a nondescript brown color and he kept it short, leaving just enough to stick out in all directions, making him look like he'd just gotten out of bed most of the time. His beard, on the other hand, was huge and bushy, and covered most of his face and all of his neck. Eli never knew exactly what Danny looked like, except for his eyes, which were always friendly. If Danny's beard had ever been trimmed, there was no sign of it, and it seemed to grow into and out of his mouth, ears, and nose. Besides the beard, Danny always wore bib overalls, even when he and Maud came to visit Rick and Eli in Los Angeles. A faded T-shirt, with some illustration or saying hidden under the overalls, and Birkenstock sandals rounded out Danny's outfit.

The second of the big differences between the brothers was in their automobiles. Rick kept his fire-engine red '67 Cadillac convertible clean enough to eat off. Eli knew better than to leave even a gum wrapper in that Caddy. Even the inside of the trunk was spotless in Rick's car.

Danny wasn't so particular. The old International was so filthy that it appeared to be held together by the dirt. In the back where he had to put his things for the ride to the farm, Eli saw beer cans, a starter motor, bones, rusty tools, a couple of empty gas cans, and more—an unbelievable assortment of junk. Eli was afraid to put his guitar in that mess but he had no choice. He tried to wedge it between two suitcases so it would stay as clean as possible. Eli had never seen so much junk or a dirtier truck than Danny's. When he finally got in the cab he found that there were several holes in the floorboards that showed the road beneath. The inside of the truck was no tidier than the back. Old paperbacks, magazines, and wrappers were piled all over the metal dashboard. The floor was littered with beer and pop cans, newspapers, greasy rags, oilcans, and other junk Eli couldn't even recognize. The seat was more springs than covering, and covered with grime.

After he helped Eli get his stuff secured in the back, Danny jumped in the driver's side and pulled the door shut with a crash that rattled everything in the poor old truck. He started asking questions in his friendly way at the same time he started the pickup. Eli feebly tried to answer the questions as he watched, fascinated, while Danny went through the routine of getting the truck going. First he pumped the gas pedal over and over. Then, still pumping, he turned the key, which caused a very slow grinding of the engine. Very slow. Eli thought it must be dead. Great, he thought. Stranded forever in Moffett. But a look at Danny's face showed him that nothing apparently was wrong. After quite a long time of this furious pumping and painfully slow grinding of the starter, the engine exploded into life with a noise that lifted Eli six inches off the seat. No muffler.

Danny smiled and nonchalantly searched for reverse, revving the engine so loudly that the sound echoed all over Moffett. Danny finally found reverse, checked the mirror, and the truck lurched into the street. Danny found first gear while they were still moving pretty fast backward, and the old green truck shot down the street in a cloud of blue smoke and dust, throwing Eli hard against the rear window.

I guess I'm in Oregon, he thought.

It took about twenty minutes to get from the bus station to Danny and Maud's farm. Most of the trip had been on a gravel road and the white dust swirled up and around everything, covering Eli and his belongings with a fine white powder. Oh well, Eli thought to himself, just something else to get used to. He had promised himself all the way here in the bus, and especially on the way out from Moffett in the pickup truck, that he was going to try to fit in. He'd make the most of it and have fun. Not like the last time.

When he and Rick had come here a few years ago, right after Eli's mother had split, Eli had felt pretty bad about things, maybe a little sorry for himself, and had spent the entire visit complaining and telling everyone how wonderful he was. Not real cool. He had the sickening feeling when he and Rick left that Danny and Maud were not sorry to see him go.

This was going to be different. He was going to be interested in Oregon this time, ask questions about the farm and the town, Moffett. Maybe he'd get to know a few kids, although if any kids lived around Danny's place, there was no sign of it. Danny and Maud sure didn't have any kids. Because of the accident, he knew.

Maud came out on the porch. She waited there, that special smile on her face that Eli remembered so well, a peaceful smile, probably the deepest, quietest smile Eli had ever seen. She leaned against the metal crutches, her body twisted slightly to the left, as always, waiting.

Danny and Maud had been in a terrible automobile accident on the freeway when they had lived in Los Angeles. Eli was two when it happened. He only remembered hearing about it later. No one talked about the accident now. Eli remembered only that Danny had been racing another guy in his Corvette when he lost control somehow and hit an overpass. Rick said that Danny was a lot different in those days than he was now. Nobody thought Danny and Maud were going to live, but they both did. When Maud recovered enough to get around, they packed up and moved to Oregon, to Moffett, to this ramshackle old farmhouse.

Eli figured that somehow the car wreck that almost killed them was what made Danny and Maud the way they were. They had a special understanding between them, like they knew a secret no one else could ever understand.

"Hi, Eli. Good to see you." Maud said, in her usual quiet way. Sincere, but quiet. "You hair sure has gotten long—it's real pretty. Come on in, we've got a room all fixed up for you."

Now at this house, Maud was in charge of all things related to making it and keeping it a home. If it was cutting wood or working on the truck or painting, that was Danny's department. But cooking, cleaning, sewing, and taking care of everything inside the house itself—Maud was in charge there. That seemed pretty old-fashioned to Eli, but that was the way Danny and Maud seemed to like it and that was the way it was. So when it was time to show Eli to his room, it was Maud that showed the way, moving with surprising

16

grace on her crutches, her bent body swinging lightly from side to side. Danny and Eli followed slowly behind.

Eli's room, his new home, was small but cozy. There was a window that looked out upon the backyard, which was almost completely covered by an enormous laurel bush, so that the bedroom was shady and cool and dark. Opposite the window was a closet that was as wide as the room itself. Against one wall was a single bed with a metal headboard, and next to the bed, under the window, was a small table. There was a rickety-looking chair in the corner. Nothing else. Except the poster. Maud must have thought the room looked a little bare for a boy's bedroom, so she'd dug out a poster from her college days and tacked it to the wall. The corners were torn off and a rip across the top had been taped. A host of little holes showed where the poster had been taken down and put up again in every dorm room and living room of a much younger Maud's life. It was a Rainier Beer poster, one of the first. It showed a forest of huge trees. Many of the trees had been cut down leaving giant stumps. The trees around the stumps on the edges of the poster were still standing. Little animals were poking their heads out from all around in the trees to see what was going on. Some had their paws over their ears. Standing on the stumps were five loggers. Except they had taken off their checked jackets and hard hats and were wearing bright-colored, tight-fitting outfits and they were holding their chain saws and double-bitted axes like guitars. One guy was playing a stump like a drum set. At the bottom of the poster it said, MAKE YOUR OWN KIND OF MUSIC. RAINIER BEER. Eli had never seen anything like it.

"Hope this is all right, Eli. It's probably a lot different than what you're used to," Danny said.

Eli thought of his black vinyl and chrome waterbed, his television; he thought of the minirefrigerator Rick had bought for his twelfth birthday. He sighed.

"This is great," he said. "I've never seen walls painted like that. That's real interesting. Did you do all of that yourself?" Eli directed the question to Maud, since she was the artistic one.

He saw Danny and Maud look at each other and smile that smile. They sort of shrugged their shoulders together, then Maud said, "Eli, that's wallpaper. Haven't you ever seen it before? You just buy it in a roll and glue it to the wall. We put that in here about a year ago. We put it in our bedroom, too."

"Jeez, I thought you guys painted all those little flowers yourself."

Danny laughed. "You city boys! Boy, I can see you have a lot to learn about the country." He was still chuckling. "Put your stuff away and get the room the way you want it. I'm going to go do chores. You can come find me when you're ready."

After Danny had gone, Maud said again, "It's nice to have you here, Eli. I just know you're going to love

18

it. If you need anything, holler. I'll be in the kitchen. We ate a late breakfast, but I bet you're starved. Lunch will be ready whenever you are.''

Eli watched her swing down the hall on her crutches and heard her humming a little song under her breath. It had been a long time since someone had mothered him. Eli thought he could probably learn to like anything if Maud was around.

3

People call you names
People never care
People never see beyond
The way you cut your hair

Living in a crazy world
They hide behind the smile
Who can find the real you?
It's enough to drive you wild

Eli enjoyed every minute of his summer with Danny and Maud. Until Tuesday, five days after he arrived.

Here was Eli, the ultimate California rock-and-roll kid, with his hair, his diamond earring, his T-shirt collection, tight jeans, a couple of pairs of fancy boots, shades, even a custom pool cue. Here was Southern California Cool dropped square into the heart of the heart of rural, small town Oregon.

Quite a contrast.

Problem was, Eli didn't know that yet. Of course, he'd had that little episode with Mr. Suspicious at the Greyhound place but he'd dealt with problem adults like that before.

And then he'd been hanging around with Danny and Maud for five days and they had been real nice and had pretty much let him be himself. They had insisted that he keep his room in fairly good order and that he keep his guitar and stereo down, but that was cool, he didn't mind. There were headphones.

He'd been enjoying doing things outside with Danny. He'd even shoveled manure from the barn three times, and he fed the chickens. Danny let him ride the little Honda dirt bike around in the hills whenever he wanted to and Eli thought that was just great. It wasn't long before he had quite a course laid out for himself through the pastures and the trees. Eli figured that riding the dirt bike and learning to help around the place was going to help him forget that there was no TV.

At first he couldn't believe it when Maud told him the TV was gone. "We just got tired of it, Eli, and we gave it away," she had said.

No TV! The last time he came here he could at least watch game shows and old movies during the long afternoons. It wasn't like the seventy-some channels he and Rick had at home, but it was television. Now even that was gone.

Well, Eli wasn't about to pout and act like a kid.

21

Secretly, though, he wondered how long he could stand it without TV. It seemed to him as though part of his life was gone without it.

But he was keeping pretty busy, and in the evenings after supper when Danny and Maud would sit and talk quietly out on the front porch or go for a walk down to the creek, Eli would write songs.

For several years Eli had been in the habit of writing a song every day, based on what had happened to him. Some of these he liked, many he did not, but he kept them all in his notebook just the same.

About eleven o'clock on the fifth day after Eli arrived, Danny found him in the pasture behind the old barn, working on the dirt bike.

"What are you doing to my bike, Eli?" asked Danny in his good-natured, easygoing way. He had a way of letting Eli know when he was doing something wrong, or when he didn't really appreciate something Eli was doing, without getting all over him about it. Danny always smiled and talked in that gentle way. Eli couldn't imagine him getting angry. Eli was used to Rick, who had a pretty short fuse and got angry easily. Just the same, Eli got the message from his uncle that he shouldn't be fooling with the bike. At least not without asking.

"Aw, nothing. I just wanted to look at the carburetor to see if I could get some more air to this thing. She doesn't seem to run up hills too great. Cuts out, you know?" The tools on the grass under the bike and the grease on Eli's face and hands said that he had been doing more than looking. Danny just grinned.

"Let's have a look. When did you become such a mechanic? You seem like a guy who wouldn't know the difference between a carburetor and a piece of celery."

Eli didn't take offense. He knew Danny was just talking. He decided not to tell Danny that he really had no idea what he was doing, just a vague notion that more air might make the old bike go a little faster. Eli knew that air came through the carburetor.

"We can adjust these throttle screws here, that might help. What in the world did you have this off for? That's the valve cover. I suppose you were trying to get more air to the valves, too." Danny laughed. "Looks like she could use a new air filter, though. We can get one in town." He was still grinning and Eli decided that he wasn't angry about the Honda. In fact, he thought Danny looked pleased. "Get that old thing put back together and clean up. We'll go to town after lunch and get a few things. Then we'll go swimming."

In Los Angeles, when Eli and his friends wanted to go swimming, they went down to Jackson Swimming Center, paid $1.50, and mostly lay around and watched the girls get tan. In Oregon, swimming meant finding a good deep hole in a river and getting into it. After Danny and Eli had picked up a new air filter and a few other things for the bike in Moffett, Danny headed for the local swimming spot, which was in the opposite direction from the house and about ten miles out of town.

The old truck followed the pavement for a while, then turned off onto a dirt road that was barely visible from the highway. To get to this swimming hole, you really had to know where you were going. The dirt track wound among the trees for about a mile, the truck whining slowly in first gear. Eli could see the dust, thick on the leaves of the plants and trees along the roadside. People must come here often, he thought. Finally the firs and salmonberry turned into willows and long grass and Eli could smell something different in the air. After a minute they came out of the brush and up over a bank and there was the river. Danny drove right through the water, crossed the river in the shallows and continued up the opposite bank where a small faint road was visible between two big patches of blackberry bushes. They were on a kind of peninsula, on the inside of a bend in the river and Eli thought it was one of the prettiest places he had ever seen.

Tall fir trees stood just far enough from each other to provide a canopy of shade. Between the firs, soft green grass grew, and here and there lay big moss-covered rocks. It looked like a park. The truck jounced across the grass and stopped in the parking area for the swimming hole. Eli counted seven other vehicles already parked there—one old Chevy Impala and six pickup trucks. Danny had said not too many people knew about this spot and after the long and confusing

24

trip in, Eli could see why. He was very surprised to see others there. Danny didn't seem to be bothered at all.

Eli was wearing some shocking pink, green, and orange fluorescent baggy shorts he had brought from home and the thongs Danny had bought for him in Moffett. He followed Danny down the short trail to the river's edge. At first Eli didn't notice anything about the people sitting around on the rocks by the river. He was more interested in the swimming hole itself. He had never seen anything like it. Where the river curved back on itself in a sharp bend, it became very deep and green and still. Eli had not imagined that the shallow rippling river he had seen earlier could possibly look like this. It gave him chills up and down his spine. There was something sinister about this dark green water rolling slowly, noiselessly by him. On the side where he stood, Eli could see the water get deep very quickly as the rock bank fell away below his feet. He could see several places where divers could stand and pitch themselves into the water five feet below. A log that had washed down the river one winter jutted out over the water and had been cut with a chain saw to form a primitive diving board.

Across the river the bank rose forty or fifty feet straight up from the water. Near the waterline grew some brush and berry vines. Above those the bank was sheer rock. Fine lines showed paths where swimmers had climbed the bank to various diving points, one just above the brush and others all the way to the very top of the bluff, high above the water. Eli raised his eyes to that point, then looked at the green water flowing almost silently below. He shivered.

As a second spasm of shivering prickled his back it occurred to Eli that it was not only the height of the cliff in front of him and the seemingly bottomless green swimming hole that was affecting him. There was something else.

The twenty or so people sitting on the rocks were staring at him. All of them.

Every single one of them.

These were what Maud called Moffett Types. By that she meant people who had a very limited knowledge of the outside world and spent nearly all of their time, money, and energy trying to be exactly like their friends. Eli hadn't understood exactly what a Type was, only that Maud didn't care for them and maybe was a little scared of them.

Looking at them now, Eli did not think of his earlier conversations with Maud and he did not recognize these people as Types, but he did feel strange. Eli found himself looking downriver to the place where Danny had gone to relieve himself and wishing he would return.

There were four distinct groups at the swimming hole. The group closest to Eli was the largest and rowdiest. There were six men and six girlfriends. The men worked in the woods as loggers and because of some mechanical failure had Monday and Tuesday off this week. This was their chance to get loose and forget about work and their everyday world. This was a group that did everything together, and during the summer they liked to camp at this swimming hole and have a big time.

Having a big time meant first and foremost drinking beer. Other fun activities included riding their three-wheelers around, drinking some more beer, then shooting at frogs and turtles with their deer rifles, drinking beer, then jumping from the bluff across the river, yelling and screaming, playing their portable stereos, wrestling around with each other, sometimes taking their clothes off. No matter what else, they always drank lots of beer and made lots of noise.

When Eli and Danny arrived that afternoon this group was surprisingly mellow. They were all dressed, more or less, and the music had been turned off temporarily. They had just finished a swim and were relaxing on the sand, upriver from where Eli stood on the rocks, drinking cans of beer. When Eli turned to look at them, a couple of the women turned away, as though pretending not to see him, and giggled, but the men just stared openly. One man, a tall sandy-haired guy with a droopy mustache, said something to the others and they all laughed. Eli thought he heard the word *faggot*. He thought he had heard the tall guy say something like: "We'll fix that faggot."

"Hey, baby." Blond Mustache was talking to Eli. Eli turned back toward the water and pretended to ignore him. He knew that with a group of rowdies like these a smart retort or a raised finger might easily lead to trouble so he simply stared out over the water. Eli felt his jaws clenching and his face and neck getting hot. When was Danny coming back?

"Hey, chicky. I'm talking to you!" Macho Man was yelling louder now. Other people who had at first stared at Eli and then gone about their business were now quietly waiting to see what was going to happen.

"Honey, I can see you ain't got no little boobs yet but there still ain't no topless sunbathing on this beach. This ain't France you know." Big laughs from the men. Nervous giggles from some of the girlfriends. "Sure do have pretty hair though. Real nice hair." Chuckles. Another man, a tough-looking short guy with a dark crew cut, joined in the fun.

"You know, Frank, this is real embarrassing to me to be here with all these nice ladies and to see this young girl over there without no top on. You'da thought her mama woulda taught her better." The short man sighed, real big so everyone could hear. "I guess it's this new generation, you know, I just don't know what this world is coming to."

The first man hadn't taken his pale blue eyes off Eli. He wasn't laughing like everyone else. "Maybe this little girl is deaf. I don't see her paying no attention to what I'm saying. I guess I'm going to have to go help her out. Jane, do you have an extra suit?" Jane was a short blond in a skimpy green bathing suit. She rummaged through a pile of clothing, then held up a handful of pink cloth. She giggled and handed it to Frank. "Yeah,"—he smiled—"this little bikini will be great." Blond Mustache had the tiny pink bikini in his hand. He brushed the sand from his cutoffs and took a last long pull on his beer. "Anyone want to go help me put this here bathing suit on that little girl over there?" Frank was striding toward Eli before the others had a chance to answer.

4

Swirling, swirling
Falling away
The green river death
Almost got you today

You can soar like an eagle
But you'll drop like a stone
When it's the green river death
You'll have to go it alone

Blond Mustache was about halfway to Eli and the others were beginning to follow when Danny came quietly up from behind and stood between Eli and the group.

The six men came on and stopped about ten yards away.

"What's going on here," demanded Danny in his quiet, strong voice.

Eli could sense the resentment Frank felt at being

30

thwarted in front of his buddies. He saw him search Danny up and down, trying to decide what to do. Saw his facial muscles twitch and his jaw clench. Frank's hand on the ball of cloth that was the pink bikini was white. His icy blue eyes went quickly from Danny to Eli then back to Danny again.

"Why, boys, this a here 'pears to be a boy; 'taint no girlie 'tall." Blond Mustache was talking in a real exaggerated southern drawl. He wasn't smiling and he wasn't looking around at his friends behind him. "We wuz jest comin' over to give this here swimmin' suit to what we all thought wuz a little girl. Jest tryin' to be neighborly, ya know. Well, fellers, I guess we done made us a mistake." The group of men turned and began walking back to the sandy area where they were camped. Frank stopped and turned around about halfway. "Y'all want a cold beer, c'mon over, y'hear?" That got big laughter from the group.

Danny put his hand on Eli's shoulder. "Don't let those turkeys get you down. They're just trying to have a good time. You just happened to get in their way. They're harmless," he said. With his hand still on Eli's shoulder, he guided him down to the rocks above the deep water. "Let's go in."

Danny peeled off the overalls and the T-shirt and, balancing for a moment on the rocks in his faded red gym shorts, dived into the green water. He made a deep dive, looking like a meteor trailing a long stream of white bubbles, and came up halfway across the river.

Without looking at Eli, Danny struck out for the opposite bank. Eli watched as he crawled out of the water and climbed gingerly in his bare feet to a spot about one-third of the way up the bluff. He stood there, scratching his belly, which hung over the shorts, looking down at the water twenty feet below. Eli glanced quickly in the direction of Macho Frank and company and found that they were watching Danny, too. So were most of the other people who were sitting around. Watching the diver seemed to be the thing to do here, Eli decided. Suddenly Danny made his dive, nothing fancy, just falling headfirst into the water with a big splash. When he came up he was smiling and turned immediately for the bluff to dive again. Several men took off their T-shirts and swam across to join him.

Eli had somehow lost interest in swimming. The incident with Mr. Macho and the pink bikini was going around and around in his head. He couldn't remember when he had felt so bad. First the jerk in the bus station and now this. His face still burned with anger and embarrassment. What was the matter with these people? Hadn't anybody in Oregon ever seen long hair before? Eli knew that he stood out from any crowd because his hair was so straight and almost platinum blond and because he was so tall for his age and so slender. But he had always wanted that. In California more was better. And no one had ever bothered him. Sometimes he got a few stares, especially when he had left Los

Angeles to travel with Styletto, but nobody had ever said anything. Lots of guys had hair this long.

As he looked around at the people at the swimming hole, though, he saw nobody with much hair at all. Eli tried to see himself as these people might see him and he realized that he did look different, but who cared? Why was it so important that everyone look the same?

He felt angry. And scared. He wouldn't admit the scared part to himself; Eli thought he was pretty tough. But he was plenty mad, he knew that. He looked at Mr. Macho sitting with three girls, making them all giggle. What a jerk, Eli thought. He wished he was back in Los Angeles with Rick. Real bad. He had grown tired of this Oregon stuff already and it wasn't even July yet. He looked at the river.

Then, out of the corner of his eye, Eli saw Frank dive into the river. He couldn't help noticing the smoothness of the dive; hardly a ripple as he entered the water. As Frank was crawling out on the other side, Eli saw Danny dive from a point about halfway up the bank, spread his arms and arch his back as though he were flying, and enter the water with a hollow thump, with the sound a rock makes when it hits deep water. He swam almost the width of the swimming hole underwater and came up blowing air about ten feet in front of Eli. Three quick strokes and he was climbing out.

"Hey, how come you're not coming in? You said you were a good swimmer." Danny was a little out of breath. He looked at Eli as he dried himself. "Look, I told you not to let those punks bother you, they don't mean anything. Those guys are just full of beer, showing off."

Eli had not known that his thoughts showed through so well. "Aw, they're not bothering me," he lied. "I'm just looking around this place. I've never seen anything like it. Water cold?"

Danny was getting settled on a towel; he was going to get a little sun. He shook his head. "No, just at first but you get used to it. If you go off the other side watch those rocks down at that end." He pointed without opening his eyes or lifting his head. "Any of those spots down there you gotta make sure you clear a couple of rocks that stick out. You can see them, just be careful."

Eli looked across the river. Blond Mustache was still climbing the bluff. He was climbing slowly in his bare feet, looking for solid footing. He was past the spot where Danny had just been, heading for an outcropping not too far from the top of the bank. A couple of swimmers had dived already, from lower points, and were climbing out to join the others who were watching Frank. Soon everyone at the swimming hole, except Danny, who was asleep, was watching tall, muscular Frank climb the bluff. He seemed to be used to being watched.

When he reached the outcropping, he sat down and hung his legs over the edge, swinging his feet and smiling. His friends were shouting encouragement. Eli did not see any trail going upward from the rock on which

Frank sat. This then was the highest diving point. From the way the people were talking, Eli gathered it was seldom that anyone dived from it.

Suddenly Frank stood up. He looked right at Eli, as if to say, "Watch this, baby." As he left the rock, Frank seemed to float in air, like a butterfly, arms outstretched, body arched and perfectly horizontal to the water. Eli heard a collective gasp from the onlookers and found himself holding his breath. Frank soared out above the sparkling green water, did a neat little somersault, tucked, and entered the river without a splash. A perfect dive. Eli whistled quietly. He had never seen anyone dive so well.

When Frank came up his friends gave him a round of applause. He joined them on the sand and opened another beer, a returning, victorious hero. There were a few glances toward Eli, as though this feat was somehow for his benefit, and then the group settled into their usual routine, talking, laughing, playing the portable stereo, drinking.

Eli slid down the steep bank and slipped noiselessly into the water. He wasn't sure what he was going to do but he found himself swimming steadily for the opposite bank. The water was cold and felt strange rushing by him and under him as he swam. He imagined the bottom of the river to be far below him. He tried to see it by putting his face in the water but could only see shadows and light.

When he reached the other side he sat for a minute

on the bank next to the water, below the brush. There was a beer can in the water near his foot. He wondered what kind of person would bother to bring beer clear across the river.

He noticed that several people had seen him and were pointing and talking. Eli began to climb the bluff. The rocks were sharp and crumbly and he was forced to climb slowly and test every step before he shifted his weight to that foot. He passed the first two diving spots and was soon at what seemed to be the place most divers used. The path was fairly well established and the outcropping of rock was worn smooth from hundreds, maybe thousands, of feet.

Eli stood on the rock and looked down at the water. He was amazed at how high he was. This was the place from which Danny had made his first dive. From where Eli had been sitting across the river it had not appeared to be any great height. From here, it seemed an incredibly long fall, and into water with no visible bottom. Eli felt his knees weaken.

He returned to the path and continued climbing upward. He passed two more diving spots but did not stop to look. By now he could see the people below staring up at him. He felt as though he were on top of a mountain. He could see the cars parked behind the beach area and the road leading off through the fir trees and the green grass. He could see the river in both directions, could see that it became shallow again on both ends of the swimming hole. Far in the distance he could see blue mountains, hazy and shimmering in the heat. Still he climbed.

Soon he was sitting on the rock from which Frank had flown not too long before. Eli looked at the people across the river. They seemed to be as much below him as across from him. He felt as though he would land right on top of them if he jumped out far enough. He could not see the edge of the water below, it was hidden beneath the bluff. The distance to the water was overwhelming. Eli felt dizzy when he looked down, so he kept his gaze out in front of him.

He hadn't really thought about what he would do when he got here. He had started climbing automatically and kept going and now here he was. He supposed he would have to jump into the river. It looked almost impossible to climb back down without falling. After the warning Danny had given him about the submerged rocks he didn't want to just slide in by accident.

It was an awful long drop.

As he stood up to jump, Eli saw Blond Mustache and two of his buddies dive into the water and strike out for the bluff. It was interesting to see people swimming from above, he thought. He noticed that they left a trail of foamy bubbles behind them. He couldn't jump until they crossed over because there was a slight breeze and it was hard to predict where he might land in the river. If he landed on someone in the water, he was pretty sure it would kill them both.

The three men crossed the river quickly and Eli

waited for them to begin climbing. He wouldn't be able to see them until they reached the first diving rock because of the way the bluff curved outward from the water. Eli sat down and hugged his knees to his chest. He was starting to shiver. He wanted to fling himself into the water and get it over with; waiting up here made him nervous. Where were those guys?

After several minutes of waiting, it became apparent that they weren't climbing up the bluff. Maybe they just want to sit by the water, Eli thought. He decided it was now or never. He picked up a fist-sized rock from behind him and lobbed it out into space so that it followed the path his body would take when he jumped. He watched it plummet and splash into the river below. The splash was almost hidden from view but it sounded like deep water. Eli could see he would have to throw himself far out from the bank if he wanted to clear the rocks with any margin of safety.

He stood on the extreme edge of the flat diving rock and curled his toes for a better grip. He leaned out over the water, too late to come back now, bent his knees, and pushed off with his feet. As he left the rock he forced himself to look straight ahead and not down at the water. He did not want to hit flat, not from this height. Fear left him as he committed himself to his flight and Eli felt himself smiling, falling, flying. He stretched his arms over his head as the water rushed up at him. He slipped into the green river feet first, toes pointed, fingers locked, straight as an arrow; a graceful diver in reverse.

The sudden quiet of the deep water after the rush of the air past his ears was the first thing Eli noticed, then the surprise of his feet lightly touching the bottom. He had supposed somehow that the river was bottomless but here he was, standing on a sandy underwater knoll. He could see the top of the river far above him, the bank stretching steeply away. It was an exhilarating moment, knowing he had been successful in his jump, that he hadn't gotten hurt, that the creeps who had called him a girl earlier had seen him go off the highest part of the bluff and do it well.

As he was getting ready to push off from the sandy bottom, Eli heard three splashes, one, two, three, directly above his head. He remembered the three men swimming across the river as he had waited on the rock far above. He looked up to see them racing downward, straight toward him, trailing bubbles. They were wearing face masks and flippers.

Eli was not sure what was going to happen but he didn't like this at all. He pushed off quickly and began ascending, trying to swim away from the three approaching men. He was running out of air and the three men could easily outswim him. Their greater strength and the flippers gave them a tremendous advantage. Eli could see that they were going to intercept him about halfway to the surface. He tried to swim past them, but they formed a ring around him quickly. Eli saw Frank's face through the mask as he reached out, put one hand on each of Eli's shoulders and pushed him down hard toward the bottom of the river. Eli's heart pounded as he tried to maneuver around the men. He had no air left. Once again, Frank shoved Eli downward, away from the air he so desperately needed.

Eli was panic-stricken now. He knew he had only a few seconds before he would pass out. Already his head was throbbing and everything was starting to look gray and dim. The three men were tangled above him, there was no way to get past them. He felt his arms go out and his hands fill with flesh, then nothing.

5

When it gets real bad
You're gonna fall, fall, fall
They say the story's sad
And that is all, all, all

Running for the trees
So you can hide, hide, hide
You gotta find your soul
And put it back inside

Eli awoke and stared without moving at the trees that rose from the earth under his body and soared infinitely into the pale blue sky. There was no sound, no movement, and as he lay very still, Eli knew that something was different, there was something new he was supposed to remember. But there was nothing in his mind. Nothing.

He raised his head just a little to look around, then put it back down. He saw that he was wearing Levis

41

and boots and a flannel shirt. The shirt was strange, he had never seen it before. He was lying at the edge of a clearing on soft green grass; lying on his back under some very large trees. He recognized them as fir trees, the kind that grow all over Oregon.

Oregon. Eli started to remember. He lay looking up at the trees and let his mind search around without him, as though his brain and he were disconnected. He thought of the seek function on the stereo at home. In Los Angeles. It looked for a station, found it, and then went on to the next station unless someone stopped it. That was what Eli's mind was doing. He was separated from his mind and it was working for him, trying to find something. Eli didn't care whether it found anything or not.

Oregon. He rememberd now he was in Oregon. That was strange. He lived in California, in Los Angeles. What was he doing out here? But then, as though insisting that he remember everything, his mind began showing him pictures, vivid pictures, in some kind of order. It was as though there were another person inside him, telling him a story, forcing him to remember.

Eli continued to lie face up in the grass and let the pictures flash across his consciousness.

He saw a picture of Rick, his father, crying in a crowded bus station. Then the scene changed and Eli was on a bus, looking out over the endless fields of central California as night fell. The scenes were coming faster now. Eli still didn't truly understand the story but he knew it was important to try to put it together. He knew now that he must remember. He felt grateful to his mind for helping him.

He was on a bus, early in the morning, just waking up. The freeway was smaller now, two lanes each way. It was almost empty. Eli remembered being surprised by how few cars there were. The fields were green instead of brown and the mountains that held them were blue and very close. This must be Oregon, he thought.

Scene: A little town in the distance, out the bus window. A river next to the road. Cows in the fields. Barbed-wire fences.

Scene: The Greyhound pulling away with a roar and a cloud of diesel smoke. A knowing wave from the driver.

Scene: A skinny stupid man in a uniform scowling, a speck of white spit on his lip as he talks.

Scene: An old, dirty, pickup truck pulling into a parking spot, a big, burly, bearded guy in overalls jumping out, running . . . Danny.

Now it all came at once. In a flood of understanding, Eli remembered moving into the shady little bedroom, working around the farm. He remembered going to the Western Auto store for parts for the bike, then the ride to the swimming hole.

The swimming hole. He had jumped off the highest rocks into the dark water and those three guys had waited for him on the bank, then come after him. He remembered his panic when he couldn't get past them to breathe. He had felt strange then. Calm, cold. He had seen colors, like rainbows but really bright, like the test pattern on the television. Then bull's-eyes. There had been music, strange, like a synthesizer, like nothing he had ever heard before. Mostly Eli remembered how calm he had suddenly felt, how peaceful. Then he had been angry when a strong hand gripped his upper arm and pushed hard, real hard; angry when he broke the surface of the water. There was choking and gagging— he remembered the burning feeling in his throat. He had thrown up.

It was all there now. He didn't have to remember it in pieces anymore. It was like his memory had been shattered and now it was whole again. He recalled the taunting laughter of the three men while they watched Danny help Eli to the bank and gather their things to go.

The laughter he remembered most of all. As though it were some kind of game and Eli had lost. It was a big joke to them. Eli couldn't understand that. He had nearly died and they thought it was funny.

And then Danny. He hadn't said a word all the way home. Eli had tried to thank him but it sounded kind of corny, like an old movie, so he hadn't said much. When they got to the house, Maud had supper ready. Eli couldn't eat but he did drink lots of water. After a while they had started talking about it and the more they talked, the more it seemed to Eli that Danny was no different than the creeps at the river.

It wasn't like he was glad Eli had nearly drowned. But he wasn't taking the whole thing seriously. Eli remembered saying that those three ought to be shot and Danny kind of got angry, like Eli was out of line for suggesting such a thing. Then when Eli tried to insist that Danny call the police, Danny refused and kept saying it was just a little prank. A prank!

"Yeah," Danny had said, "they were just giving you a hard time and it got away from them. They didn't mean to hurt anyone."

Eli couldn't believe it. Those idiots had tried to kill him and Danny was siding with them. He felt hot tears come to his eyes and heard himself screaming, yelling and swearing at Danny. He saw the shocked look on the faces of Danny and Maud.

He had run out of the house wearing Maud's flannel shirt that she had given him before dinner and had finally ended up here in this grove of big trees. Even with his memory back in place, he couldn't recall exactly where he was. He had run down the gravel road away from the house, away from Moffett. He had run until he was exhausted. Eli did not know how far he had come or where he was or how long he had been there.

Only that this was exactly where he needed to be.

* * *

He sat up and looked around. Surrounding him was a forest of massive trees. Eli thought of pictures of the redwoods in northern California. These trees weren't redwoods but they were very big trees. The huge firs created a green canopy high overhead. The big branches swayed gently in the breeze, back and forth, making a soft rustling. A nearly imperceptible music. Underneath the canopy grew all kinds of smaller vegetation. Here and there were patches of grass and moss like the one Eli had slept on; islands in the dark green leafy undergrowth.

Eli could hear the tinkling of a small creek somewhere near him and birds making their music above him. From time to time a great rush of air swept through the forest and rustled all the leaves together, making a tremendous roar. Then everything grew calm and still again. Everything except the incessant murmur of the big firs and the hollow singing of the creek.

Eli had heard a car go by a while before. He hadn't been absolutely positive that it was a car, it might have been something else. But now the unmistakable sound of tires crunching on gravel was coming back toward him. He was rather surprised to hear sounds of civilization. He had not thought of a road being so near. He had hoped that he was hundreds of miles from anywhere.

"Eli!" It was Maud. She was driving slowly along the road, honking the horn of her little Toyota and yelling his name. "Eli! Come home, Eli!"

He didn't know what to do. Obviously he couldn't stay here forever. He couldn't go home to Los Angeles; Rick was already on the road by now. He was still pretty mad about Danny's attitude but really more embarrassed than anything else. Besides, this was Maud. He knew she was alone because if Danny was with her he would have been driving his truck. He never drove the car. Eli figured that if anyone could get things straightened out, Maud could. She was his best chance.

So he stepped out of the forest onto the gravel road just as Maud came around a bend. She stopped and he got into the passenger seat of the dirty little car just as if he had planned the whole thing to happen that way.

"Hi, Maud," he said.

"Eli," she said, nuzzling her head against his neck, her arm around his shoulder. Eli always liked that about Maud, the way she hugged him. Like a grown-up, like a lover. She never held him and squeezed him like he was a little boy. Her hugs were real. "Eli, where have you been? I've been so worried about you."

"Aw, Maud, I just slept in the trees there." He added, "It seemed like something I should do; I needed to think."

Maud looked at him in her quiet, knowing way, out of the sides of her eyes, her mouth barely smiling. "Eli, it was wrong what those guys did. I understand. But I want you to try to understand Danny. I know you think

47

he was defending those guys, but he wasn't. Danny just likes to make the best of things, he doesn't like to drag things out, you know?''

Eli didn't really know, but he nodded his head a little, to keep her talking. Somehow he wanted everything to be all right. The incident at the river was starting to seem like a long time ago, like a dream.

Maud put the car in gear and it eased forward on the gravel. All the controls were on handles so that Maud could drive the car. Her feet lay useless below the seat. "Eli, look, Danny figures since you're all right, you didn't get hurt, it's best to leave it where it lies; not make a big deal out of it. That doesn't mean he's happy about what happened, you need to understand that. He jumped on those guys real hard after he helped you get to the bank, he really read them the riot act.''

"But, Maud, they tried to kill me. I thought I was going to die. Really die. You should have seen the looks on their faces.''

"I don't know, Eli. Maybe they did, maybe they didn't.'' She saw the same hurt look come into Eli's eyes that she had seen the night before. "Look, Eli, I'm not saying you didn't fear for your life. I'm only telling you that those characters probably didn't intend to drown you outright, right there in front of everyone. They were probably just giving you a hard time. There's a lot of good old boys like that around Moffett, all over Oregon. They drink too much, drive fast, do crazy stuff. They're always challenging each other to do something more dangerous, more life-threatening, than the last stunt. That's just how they are. I don't like it and you don't have to like it, but that's just how they are.

"Danny talked to the three of those guys after you ran to the truck and they seemed kind of ashamed of themselves, at least that's what he thought. They said they were just trying to have a little fun. I don't know, Eli . . ."

Maud's voice trailed off, as if she was thinking of something else but wasn't sure how to say it. Eli just waited, seeing the forest going slowly by the Toyota. That's how it was with Maud, you had to let the conversation flow at her pace.

Finally she said, "Eli, I think you ought to be careful, that's all. Danny doesn't think those rednecks meant any real harm and maybe they didn't. But he was telling me after you ran off last night about them teasing you, threatening to put a bikini on you. He told me what you told him about the guy in the bus station. Maybe nobody in Moffett would hurt you. But they don't seem to be accepting you, either."

Eli hadn't thought of it that way. To him there had been two isolated incidents. He hadn't considered that there might be more. But now he heard Maud telling him that this might not be the end of the trouble, that it might be only the beginning.

"Are you telling me I ought to cut my hair off and wear red suspenders and a cowboy hat?" Eli let a little anger creep into his voice. Maybe more than a little.

"No, Eli, not at all. I'm proud of the way you look, you know that. I'm just saying that the folks around here aren't used to boys with long hair and earrings, that's all. You might want to be careful where you go. Go with Danny and you'll be all right. Just be careful, that's all. Okay?"

"Okay. No problem. I'm going to spend all my time here at the farm anyway, so I won't be able to get in any trouble even if I wanted to." Eli was trying to make a joke, trying to smooth things over. He noticed Maud was smiling. They were pulling into the driveway now.

"Anyway, you did a pretty good job on that guy's neck." Somewhere, Eli knew what she meant. But it was too deep, too far down.

So he said, surprised, "What guy?"

Maud said, gathering her crutches from the backseat, "That one guy, the guy that tried to hold you underwater. Danny said you put a bruise the size of Texas on his neck when you grabbed him, as he tried to get away." She was grinning now, not even trying to hide it.

"I did?"

"Oh yeah. Danny said that when he got to you, in the river, you had both hands around that guy's neck and were strangling him for all you were worth. He said that old boy will be black-and-blue for weeks."

Eli grinned. He felt better all over.

That night, Danny and Maud and Eli sat around the

dinner table until well after dark, talking. Danny pretty much said the same thing as Maud, that there was no use trying to do anything about the swimming hole incident now that it was over. It would be best, he agreed, for Eli to stay close to the place and not take any chances on running into some more good old boys, at least not when he was alone. Danny told Eli that if he was going to ride the dirt bike, ride it in the other direction, away from Moffett.

"There's nothing up that road but woods," he said.

Eli looked at Maud and smiled. She hadn't told Danny where she had found Eli that morning. He thought of the enormous trees and the ferns. He thought of the little creek he had heard but hadn't seen. Eli thought he wouldn't mind exploring up that way. If it made Danny and Maud happy, that was even better.

After they had talked, Danny got out his Martin guitar and had Eli bring his guitar and amplifier into the living room to play with him. They played and sang some old folk songs, Danny and Maud doing most of the singing and Eli trying to add what he could with his guitar. At first he played too loud and harsh, but after a bit he got into a groove and started sounding pretty good. Eli could tell that Danny was impressed, which made him feel just great. They even switched guitars for a couple of songs. Danny had played electric guitar for years in Los Angeles and could still make Eli's Stratocaster sing, but the big boxy Martin was strange and unfamiliar in Eli's arms. Most of what he knew on his electric guitar sounded thin and ugly on the acoustic Martin. After he got his own guitar back, Danny wanted to sing an old spiritual called "Will the Circle Be Unbroken" to end the evening. He taught Eli the words to the chorus and it seemed to be important to him that Eli get the music just right. When they began singing the song for real, Eli found some riffs on his guitar that sounded perfect to his ear and made Danny and Maud smile at each other. On the chorus, Danny and Maud sang two harmony parts to Eli's melody. Now Eli could see why it was so important to Danny for him to get the tune just right. With the three vocal parts and the two guitars all going at once, it was like magic! Eli had never felt anything like it. He forgot all about the river and the bikini and the sour man in the bus station and just became the music. Danny even left him some room to play a few solos in between the verses and he thought he had never played better. Maud and Danny took turns singing the verses, which Eli didn't know, and then they all joined together each time the chorus came around. The song seemed to go on and on and just get better as it went. Finally, Danny signaled that it was the last chorus and they held out the last note, ending together as though they had practiced for days. Eli could not remember when he had enjoyed something so much.

As he lay in bed, waiting for sleep, he heard the laurel bush outside rustle in the breeze and scrape across the screen. He thought about the trees he had slept under the night before and how they murmured and sang so softly. Eli had really never thought about trees before. They were there, he saw them, but he hadn't *thought* about them like this. Like they were real and alive. Like they were important.

He rolled over and pulled the blanket up under his chin. The song Danny had taught him kept rolling through his head. The sound of the trees and the gurgling creek and the birds was there, too. He saw the green river sweeping below his feet as he stood on a rock, forty feet above the water. He saw Maud's flushed face as she sang, her crutches beside her on the carpet. So much seemed to have happened since he came to Oregon, so much so fast. Eli thought of Rick, who was somewhere on the East Coast, and he thought of his mother, his beautiful, strange mother who was probably gone forever.

It was like a circle, Eli thought. *Will the circle be unbroken, by and by, Lord, by and by.* He didn't really understand what that meant, but he could sense that the trees and the river and Danny and Maud and the music and all of it was somehow the circle of his life, and Eli knew, as he felt himself floating into sleep, that his circle had suddenly grown much larger.

6

You find out who you are
In the peaceful times
You find out where you are
In the peaceful times

You get to know your friends
In the peaceful times
The circle of your life grows
In the peaceful times

Danny and Maud prided themselves on taking care of their own needs in their own way. This meant, among other things, an enormous organic garden, fenced against the deer, a milk cow, a loom that Maud used to make much of her clothing, and a big, Fisher wood stove in the living room. To Eli this translated into weeding, picking vegetables, repairing fences, cleaning stalls, and splitting wood.

It was the last of these that Eli found nearly unbearable. He liked the big garden with all of its smells and textures. As he pulled and hoed the weeds, Eli learned about each kind of plant at close range. He admired the delicate yellow blossoms of the tomatoes and the huge, hairy leaves of the zucchini. Once, Maud had even had Eli pick a few of the big yellow zucchini blossoms and she had coated them with something and fried them. He had thought that a little strange but they tasted good. There was sweet corn, of course, and green beans which seemed to grow up the wire support set up for them so fast that they could almost be seen moving.

And there were things you wouldn't expect in a garden, at least Eli hadn't known about them. Like flowers. Lots of big yellow and orange and red flowers, scattered all through the vegetables. Sometimes Maud used these in salads and in cooking. And herbs. There was a whole section of the garden devoted to odd, squatty, gray green plants that Maud called herbs. Eli knew some of the names: oregano, basil, thyme, mint, sage, parsley. But he often couldn't remember which one was which. He thought the herbs smelled wonderful, and he liked to weed that part of the garden best.

Eli didn't mind caring for Matilda, the milk cow. He liked her real well. And cleaning the barn wasn't so bad once you got used to it. Painting Maud's kitchen was easy. So was fixing the fences. Eli mowed the lawn, watered the yard sometimes; once, right after his arrival, he had even helped Maud plant some flower plants in the backyard. She had called them marigolds and said that the deer wouldn't eat them. Maud had praised Eli's work and said how much help he was to her and wondered how she had ever gotten along without him around the house. Eli knew part of this was just Maud being motherly, but it was true, too, that Maud didn't get around easily, and Eli could see that he really was a big help to her. When Danny got home from the mill in the evening, Maud would tell him all the things Eli had done for her and it made him feel proud and good.

In the afternoons when there wasn't much to do and Maud was usually weaving or working in the kitchen, Eli would take off on the little Honda. It was a couple of miles up the road to the forest he had gone to that awful night after he had almost drowned in the river. Since that night, Eli had gone there nearly every day. He had discovered the creek he had only heard that night and found it to be endlessly fascinating. There were small pools where he could sit in the shadows and watch the little silver fish and water skippers dart and flash through their small worlds. He discovered a miniwaterfall and enjoyed throwing sticks in and watching them slowly float to the edge and then plummet through the white water to swirl around in the rocky pool below.

The forest, too, was full of wonder for Eli. He had never known such quiet. The big firs would murmur high overhead. Once in a while a little brass-bellied squirrel would scoot out on a limb and chatter at him. Mostly, though, there was silence. When he was among the trees, they seemed to envelop him in their different world. Whatever might be happening in Moffett, or in noisy Los Angeles, or with Rick and Styletto, or even back at the house with Maud—all of this simply disappeared for Eli each time he visited the forest he had come to love.

It wasn't so much that other parts of his life became temporarily less important or that he stopped thinking about them for a little while. That was what happened when he went to a movie or watched a good football game on television.

This was different. It was as though the everyday world really went away and there was nothing left on earth but him and this small patch of green life and the sound of the ancient trees singing and the sound of the little creek bubbling and the sound of nothing, of silence. It was always with some sadness that he walked slowly back out to the road, climbed onto the bike, took a last long look over his shoulder, kicked down the starter, and drove off toward the farm.

Today it had been more difficult than ever to leave the dark green coolness and head for the farm: Today Eli was supposed to split firewood.

He pushed the bike into the darkness of the barn and grabbed the splitting maul and his gloves. The wood was piled near the barn door. The chopping block was out in the dusty barnyard, far from any shade, and near it was the battered wheelbarrow. Eli's job was to stand the firelogs on the chopping block, one by one, and split them in half with the maul. When he had split enough to fill the wheelbarrow, he was to carry a load of split wood around to the back of the barn and stack it. Then he returned to the chopping block and started over.

The first few times Eli had tried this, with Danny, it had been fun and challenging. He had worked hard to hit the round logs in the center so they would split in two equal pieces and to hit them hard enough so they would split clean. His muscles had ached and the sweat had poured off him. Now that the blisters had become callouses and he had learned how to swing the maul so that it did most of the work for him, splitting firewood had become tedious. And the pile of unsplit wood seemed to grow larger rather than smaller.

Eli remembered with some chagrin how he had been the one to insist that the logs be split by him. He grinned a little to himself as he fixed his hair into a quick braid, put on the stiff leather gloves, and went to work.

Set up the log. *Click.*

Swing the maul. *Crack.*

Two halves roll into the dirt and the maul quivers in the chopping block. *Thunk.*

Click. Crack. Thunk.

Click. Crack. Thunk.

Maud of course could not split the wood and Danny had been complaining about how much overtime he had been putting in down at the mill, with no end in sight.

Click. Crack. Thunk.

One night at supper Danny had mentioned that he might have to hire a man to come and split the wood; he didn't see how he could get everything done before the autumn rains came.

Click. Crack. Thunk.

Eli had done what he figured any boy would have done in his situation: He'd volunteered. After all, he had been taken in for the summer.

Click. Crack. Thunk. A rhythm began to develop now.

Besides, he hadn't wanted Danny to think he wasn't man enough to do farm work. He hadn't wanted him to think he was just a city boy. Or worse. Some sort of wimp or something like those jerks at the river thought he was.

Click. Crack. Thunk.

And he hadn't wanted to seem ungrateful. "Yeah," he had said, "I can bust that wood up in no time. I'll have it done in no time, you watch." At first, Danny wasn't going to let him do it, but Eli insisted and, after several evenings of working together, Danny had to grudgingly admit that it would sure be a big help if Eli could get some of the firewood split.

Click. Crack. Thunk.

Some of it! Eli had bragged: "I'll do all of it, no problem."

Click. Crack. Thunk.

59

And now here he was. Just him and the woodpile. And my big mouth, he thought.

As Eli was returning from his eighth load and thinking to himself that maybe he ought to be splitting wood in the morning when it was cool, two unusual things happened. First, he saw a white truck drive by on the gravel road. It was rare that a car or truck he didn't recognize went by. The road didn't go anywhere, just ended about ten miles past the farm, so it was not particularly well traveled. There were two places about half a mile past the farm. They were both mobile homes owned by old people and Eli knew those cars. There was the mail carrier who went by every day in the passenger seat of a dirty green Blazer. Eli still wasn't sure how she drove from the wrong side of the car. And once in a while a car or truck cruised slowly past, looking for a swimming hole or, more often, simply looking.

But this was none of those. There was something about the white pickup that bothered Eli a great deal, but as he watched it go by he couldn't understand what it was. It had a little canopy over the rear bed, which looked to be full of some sort of equipment. There was an official-looking round seal on the door but Eli couldn't make out what it said. The two men in the cab were wearing hard hats and Eli could see that they both had short hair and trim beards. The truck went by at a slow steady speed, as though the driver knew exactly where he was going and was in no particular hurry to get there.

There was something about the speed that said much about the purpose of the men inside, and definitely something about those plastic hard hats, something that set Eli on edge. That pickup truck should not be here, he thought, but he could not understand how he knew that.

As he stood in the shade of the maple tree at the corner of the barn, still holding the empty wheelbarrow in both hands, staring after the mysterious white pickup, the telephone rang inside the house, and after a minute Maud called out, "Eli, it's for you."

Now it was real unusual for the phone to ring; Maud and Danny didn't seem to know all that many people and they didn't seem to like talking on the phone. But it was absolutely astonishing for the phone to ring and then be for Eli. He dropped the wheelbarrow so fast that it tipped over, and he ran for the back door. He ran through the cool back porch and into the house to find Maud leaning on her crutches, holding the receiver out to him, smiling that knowing Maud smile.

"It's your dad," she said. "It's Rick."

Eli felt a little funny talking to Rick on the telephone. He almost thought he was nervous about it. But he was glad to hear Rick's voice and before long he was telling Rick all about the summer and his stay in Oregon. Eli was surprised to find himself describing in great detail his jump into the river but leaving out the part about the three guys trying to hold him underwater. For some reason, he thought it best not to tell Rick about that. He did tell him about the guy in the bus station when he arrived in Moffet, when Eli figured he had at least held his own. Danny had said Eli owned a mouth that wouldn't give an inch. Rick laughed at that. "Yeah," he said, "I should have known those cowboys up there would be no match for you." Unlike Danny, Rick seemed to be unconcerned about the whole thing. Eli felt relieved.

There seemed to be something that Rick wanted to say, but he let Eli finish describing his summer. He seemed genuinely surprised when Eli told him he was splitting five cords of firewood. He was even more surprised when Eli explained that he had volunteered on his own, that it was something he really wanted to do to pay back Danny and Maud for letting him stay there. Eli wasn't sure how to tell Rick about his love for the big trees he had found and the creek and the ferns. He explained, sort of lamely, that he had fixed up a dirt bike and rode it often to a place where he could think, where he could be by himself. Rick seemed to understand that. Eli thought it strange that there were some parts of his summer he could not explain to anyone, not even to Rick. He thought of the circle of his life and how it had grown and how it was only him—only Eli—

in the center now and how there were . . . truths, truths that he alone could know, that he must be content to hold deep within and share with nobody. Thinking of the circle that his life had become reminded Eli of the gospel song he had learned to sing with Danny and Maud. That reminded him of something else.

''Hey, Rick! You should see the new guitar I got from Danny. Well, it's really his old guitar, that old Guild, remember? Yeah? He gave it to me! No, I mean, I don't think so. I think he means for good. I can keep it! I think.''

Maud was nodding her head from across the kitchen where she was cutting potatoes for supper.

''Yeah, Maud says I can have it. Isn't that great? Yeah, you ought to hear me play country music, I can really twang that thing. The Strat? Sure, I play it sometimes. But this Guild is a lot better for playing songs with Danny and Maud after supper. What? Yeah, almost every night. I even sing, can you believe it? They don't have a TV, you know. No, none. I'm getting to where I don't miss it. Write songs? Oh, sometimes. Usually I'm too tired, but I've written five or six. Yeah, I think they're pretty good. Hey, how's Styletto? You guys rockin' them hard? No kidding? Three encores? Hey I knew it! You're the best, I already knew that. Sure, I'm listening. What? Longer? Canada? How long? Well, yeah, I'm fine here. No, they're cool, I'll be all right. I wish I was with you though, seeing those crowds go crazy. You don't know how long, huh? All right. Call me when you know, all right? Yeah, I got your letters. Thanks. And thanks for calling. Here's Maud.''

Eli returned to the barn and put the splitting things away. He could see Maud still talking to Rick. She was nodding her head a lot and waving her arms; she seemed to be trying to convince him of something. He decided to go sit in the garden. He absently picked at weeds and thought about the phone call. Like the white pickup, the call bothered him and he didn't know why. He was surprised that Rick would call, he hadn't expected him to. Rick really hadn't said anything to make Eli feel unhappy. In fact, he had been full of good news. Styletto seemed to be taking the country by storm; everywhere they went the band met with unbelievable success. And now a new tour, as soon as this one was over. A short one, Rick had said, into Canada and the Midwest. Big arenas. And then home to Los Angeles. Eli didn't know exactly when that would be, but then he hadn't known before Rick called, either. So why was he feeling so unhappy, so bothered by the call?

There had been something in Rick's voice, he decided, something that was telling him more than all the words in the world could say, a note that said this: Nothing can ever be the same.

Just then the International pulled in and Maud met Danny at the front steps, something she never did, as

if she had been waiting for him, and they talked seriously, quietly, for a moment before going into the
house. Eli didn't need to hear their words to know that
something was different, and from the way they glanced
at him in the garden as they spoke he knew that something different was about him.

Listen and I'll tell you
About a secret place
Somewhere you can go
To escape the human race

Now they want to take it
Haul it all away
Turn it into gold
If they can find a way

N ow Eli had something else to think about: Rick had told Maud on the phone that his tour into Canada would last at least until the middle of October, maybe longer. Evidently he was unsure how to break this news to Eli so he asked Maud to talk to Eli for him. Eli was disappointed with his father for not telling him this, but he listened as Maud explained that Rick would be in Los Angeles for less than a week all summer—not even enough time for Eli to visit—and that Styletto's Canada concerts would really help sell records up there. "Rick," she said, "is sorry he can't be with you, but. . . ." Her hands went palm up beside her shoulders, she shrugged, and she made a questioning look with her mouth and eyes. With this gesture Maud seemed to say she wasn't sure she agreed with Rick's decision. Danny shook his head a couple of times from side to side but said nothing. She explained to Eli that he was welcome to stay as long as necessary, and she praised his work, especially the firewood he had split. Maud smiled as she told Eli that she and Danny might just keep him forever. She reached over and put her hand on Eli's wrist, stopping him from lifting his glass of milk, and caught his eyes with hers. Her hand was cool and dry. "Eli," Maud said, "we love you and love having you here." Danny nodded in agreement.

Eli listened to every word she spoke and his mind raced ahead to October. He thought about the rains Danny always mentioned and he thought about the firewood still to be split and Eli thought to himself that October was a long time to wait to see his friends again and he even tried to think what he might do in his little shady bedroom when it got cold and wet outside. But the most important thing of all about autumn never crossed Eli's mind until Danny cleared his throat, pushed himself back from the table, and spoke.

What Danny said was this: "I guess we'd better get you down to the school and get you registered so they know you're coming."

School.

The word seemed to echo through Eli's brain as though through the empty corridors of the school itself.

School was something he had not let himself consider. He had never known when he was to return to Los Angeles but not once had it occurred to him—never in his wildest dreams—that he might still be in Oregon for the start of school.

Dear Rick,

I have decided to write to you even though I know you're moving so fast the letters can't reach you where you are. I'll just send my letters to our apartment and you can read them when you get there, okay?

I'm glad you called yesterday. Maud told me that you won't be coming home until October and I'll have to stay here until then. I guess that will be all right. Maud and Danny are real nice and I'm doing all right here. I told you they don't have a TV. Well, I keep pretty busy so I don't miss it too much. Danny gave me his old guitar, did I tell you that? He says I'm getting pretty good. I play that old Guild most of the time. My electric guitar stays under the bed. I

68

don't think Maud likes it very well. Did you know
they don't eat meat? Maud is a great cook but she
makes strange things. Rice and eggplant and stuff
like that. I'm always starved here so I eat it. I guess
I told you I'm splitting their wood for them. All of it!
I bought some work boots and gloves with the money
you gave me and I'm working hard on that wood!
Danny says I look like a true Oregonian now. Except
my hair. He still teases me about it. I guess I'm the
only boy in Moffett with long hair.

Today Danny and I went to the school to sign me
up. It's pretty weird. It's an elementary school! The
schools are like that here, I guess. All kids from kin-
dergarten through eighth grade go to this one school!
It's smaller than the science wing of Fairfield. There
was only the secretary and a couple of janitors work-
ing when we went down there. Schools in the sum-
mer are strange. All of the desks were out in the
hall! The secretary looked like she thought I was
pretty strange, her eyes kept going to my earring.

Well, I'd better get some sleep. I've got wood to cut
tomorrow!

> *Love,*
> *Eli*

For three days after he had been registered at Moffet
Elementary School, Eli worked like a demon on the
woodpile. Somehow, now that he knew how long he

would be staying with Danny and Maud, the work got easier and he minded it less. He thought of the wood as belonging partly to him now and that made splitting it more fun. Eli was getting stronger and that helped, too. He had lots to think about now, and he let his mind drift as he split and hauled the wood. Slowly, the stack of firewood drying in the sun behind the barn grew larger and the pile of logs in front of the barn dwindled.

Three times in those days the small white pickup carried the two hard hats past the farm and then, after several hours, back down the gravel road toward Moffett. Each time, it went by at that strange, steady pace. Each time, Eli stopped his splitting and watched the truck go by and the dust settle. Each time, he was disturbed and didn't know why.

Each evening after splitting wood, Eli was too tired to play music or write songs. He listened to Danny play a few tunes and watched Maud work at her special loom, a loom that did not need Maud's feet to make it work. The quiet rhythm of the weaving and the soft guitar music were hypnotic, and each of the three nights Maud awakened Eli where he had fallen asleep on the floor and sent him to his room to sleep the rest of the night away.

The fourth day was Saturday and Danny, in his good-natured fashion, refused to let Eli do any work.

"No woodcutting today, no nothing," he had said. "You go ride that bike or do something else. You can go back to work on Monday if you want." Eli could tell that Danny was proud of the way he had been working.

Danny and Maud were going to go shopping for groceries and household items in Moffett. Eli decided to ride the Honda up to see his trees. He hadn't been there for over a week.

He rode slowly and looked around him as he went. On the right side of the road, the same side the farm was on, the land rose sharply and in many places deep cuts had been made in the bank in order to build the road. On this, the hill side, small trees and shrubs grew in abundance.

On the other side of the road, the downhill side, was a vast field. It was as if the little road was the dividing line between the endless plain and the tree-covered mountain. In fact, the road had been built on purpose just that way, snugly against the rise of the mountain to keep the good grazing land whole.

Eli could see the line of willow and cottonwood trees far out to his left—to the north—that traced the path of the creek, his creek, as it broadened and found its way across the plain and to the river. About a half-mile past the farm, just past the two mobile homes, the road began to climb steeply and then met the creek. For several hundred yards, the creek rushed noisily along the north side of the road and Eli could see the prairie drop away beyond it. The trees were much bigger here and shaded the road now. What was open and sun-drenched before now had become dark and cool, closed.

Suddenly the road took a sharp turn to the right, steeply, following the creek, and the field was gone completely. Giant firs grew thick on both sides of the road now. In many place huge boughs met across the road and blocked out the sky completely. Eli knew the creek flowed gently somewhere to his left but he could not see it or hear it. It was quiet here, muffled. Even the roar of the little bike seemed hushed. Today as he rolled slowly along he tried to see beyond the road, to look deeply into the incredible trees, but found only darkness. Past the straight trunks that lined the road was a secret darkness. Eli wondered what it was like in there, inside. He wondered if anyone had ever gone in to find out.

His special spot was about a mile beyond the place where the road left the prairie. Eli remembered running through this deepest part of the woods that awful night more than a month ago and being scared of what might lie within the trees. He remembered now being relieved to find that the darkness did not go on forever, that the forest opened up a bit to let some of the sky through. That was the way his place was—open mossy spaces where shafts of light broke through the big firs, where ferns and grasses grew and the creek wandered and sang openly in the sunlight.

Eli felt something was wrong before he ever saw the red ribbons. It's funny how that happens; sometimes you wake up and feel strange or queasy and then that's the day you cut your leg and have to go to the hospital for sixteen stitches. Or you begin to worry about something and you can't quite put your finger on it and later the phone rings and someone you love is sick or has been in an accident.

Eli didn't know what the bright red ribbons meant, not then, not when he came around the last bend in the gravel road and saw them stretching out in a straight line as far as he could see. Saw them fluttering in the breeze as they hung in vine maples. Saw the red ribbons stapled to the bark of towering Douglas firs. Saw numbers and arrows painted right onto the gravel at the edge of the road, painted in the same fluorescent red color, red that screamed against the cool green of Eli's trees.

He did not understand what the line of red was telling him as it clung tenaciously to the straight road and then continued like a bullet shot from a rifle, straight as a chalkline, into the forest as the road turned lazily to the right, quitting the road then and fluttering deep into the trees, scarlet.

He parked the bike, just laid it down in the road, and followed the perfectly straight path the red ribbons made. He took one from where it hung on a low branch and examined it, was surprised to find it soft and silky and made of plastic. Where the road curved away, Eli continued to follow the red line, and when it fell away into a canyon and then up the other side and seemed to simply go forever, he turned back. At the spot where

Eli had first seen the red line begin, he now saw that the ribbons made an abrupt turn into the forest, a right angle away from the road.

The red line, the soft ribbons as they hung in the trees, made a perfect corner. And inside that corner was the spot he had come to love as much as anything in the world.

Danny was stroking his beard thoughtfully as he sat on the front porch. His eyes were troubled and he stared off, far across the field on the other side of the road. Eli thought he was taking an awful long time to answer a simple question.

When Danny and Maud had returned from shopping, Eli had been waiting for them on the porch. Without even a hello he had asked Danny what the bright ribbons in his forest meant, why they were there.

Danny had put him off. "Why don't you help me get these things in the house and I'll see if I can't answer your question." So Eli had hauled paper bags into the kitchen, then helped put things in cupboards, then waited while Danny got a can of beer and came out to the porch.

Now he was looking across the field and thinking.

"Those are survey marks, Eli," he said.

"Well, what do they mean? Why would someone put those things clear up there?" Eli asked.

Danny thought about that. "When someone wants to know exactly where the boundary of his property is, he hires a professional surveyor to find it. The surveyor puts up the ribbons so the person who owns the property can see the line.''

Danny knew why the ribbons had been placed there, he had talked to a friend of his in town about it. But he knew Eli had learned to love his special place up the road and knew that somehow the change that had come over Eli this summer was hidden in the trees that he had come to call his own. Sometimes, Danny thought, it was hard to tell the truth. So he stroked his beard and tried to find the right words.

''Does a surveyor drive a small white pickup and wear a hard hat?'' Eli asked, knowing that Danny wasn't telling him everything, but not sure of the question he needed to ask.

''Yeah, he might.''

''Well, whose property is that anyway?''

Danny took a long drink from the can. ''See that field across the road? All that field as far as you can see and all along that side of the road pretty much belongs to old man Simpson. He owns more land around here than anyone else, I guess. Old Simpson is kind of a big shot around Moffett.'' Danny sort of smiled. ''Yeah, he's a big shot, all right. Just ask him.''

Danny finished the beer, then seemed to take a deep breath, like he was getting ready to do something he really didn't want to do.

''Eli, I was talking to a guy I know named Jake today in town. Jake drives a Cat, a big tractor you know?

Well now, Eli, I know how you love those trees up there. Maud tells me you go there pretty near every day. But they're gonna cut that piece, Eli. Jake told me Simpson is getting ready to log it off. That's why those red flags are there.''

Now to anyone who had been around Oregon very long, that would have been enough said. Danny thought he had given the bad news to Eli and he stood up to go in the house. But he took one look at Eli and knew he didn't understand; he looked puzzled.

"You know what I'm talking about, Eli?"

Eli did not know. He clearly understood that Danny was telling him that something awful was going to happen to his trees, but he did not know exactly what. He only shook his head.

Danny sighed and sat back down. "I guess they don't do much logging in Los Angeles, do they?" Danny's voice had a gentleness now, the gruff tone was gone.

"Eli, old Simpson has that patch of old growth sitting up there in the corner of his place—"

"Old growth?" Eli interrupted.

"Old growth means trees that have never been logged. It means that the forest is the way it has always been, before man came. That area you go hang around is all old growth, that's why the trees are so big. They've been growing right there for hundreds of years. Anyway, Simpson owns a corner of that and he's going to have the trees cut down for lumber. Where the red flags are, that's his property, that'll all be cut."

Eli was starting to understand; his stomach twisted and his head pounded. His mouth had dried up.

"How many trees will they have to cut?" he asked.

Danny went back to stroking his beard and looked again across the prairie to the mountains that were a blue haze between the earth and sky. This time he didn't turn when he spoke.

"Eli," he said, even more gently than before, "they're gonna clear-cut that piece. That means they'll go in with chain saws and machinery and cut every single tree, bush, and plant taller than six inches and haul it away. By the time the fall rains come, boy, there won't be anything left but mud."

8

Turn to the left
They won't go
Turn to the right
They don't know
What can you do
When it's all up to you?

Take it into your own hands
Yeah
Take it into your own hands
Just take it
Into your own hands

It was the kind of dream in which the real world and the dream are connected. In which the dreamer knows that some of the experience is fantasy and some is very real but can never remember which is which. It was a dream that flowed back and forth across the dreamer's mind, washing against the memory and against time like waves lapping against the rocks. This was that rare dream that brought understanding and knowledge along with the pain.

This was a dream that had to be dreamed.

Eli was watching a concert as though from backstage. He could not see the seating area, could not see the hall itself. Yet he was aware that it was completely empty, that he alone was hearing and seeing this concert. Slowly he realized that it was not a hall he was in but a forest. The canopy of branches closed off the sky and made it seem like an enormous room, but it was not a room.

It was his special place. Eli's trees.

Styletto was on stage. They were playing their usual instruments but the sound was all wrong. Instead of the jangle, thump, and boom of a rhythm-and-blues band, they were playing the sounds of the forest. Eli smiled in his dream to see Rick with his head thrown back, legs apart, and fingers dancing all over the red guitar, only to make the delicate, tinkling sound of the creek. He was amazed to notice that the creek sound was indeed music. It sounded like someone tapping on hollow wooden tubes and seemed to be saying the same thing, over and over. Eli tried to understand the words but could not.

The rest of the band made other sounds. It was difficult to tell which instrument made each sound, but it was a quiet, peaceful music that came from the tremendous stack of speakers on each side of Styletto. The band members seemed not to be surprised to hear themselves make this music.

Suddenly a change came over the band. It was no

longer Rick, it wasn't Styletto at all. It was another band. Eli tried hard to remember if his father had ever been in the dream, but now he wasn't sure, he couldn't be sure of anything.

The song was over, the men were picking up different instruments, turning knobs on their equipment, getting ready for the next number. The lead singer counted to begin the song, One, two, three . . . bang, they were right into it, this time with the roar and power of a heavy metal band.

But wait! Eli knew this singer! He covered his face with his hands, forced himself to remember. Who was it? Short blond hair, droopy mustache . . . It was Frank! The creep from the river who had tried to put a girl's bikini on him, then drown him. Eli didn't know he was a musician.

And the band, where had he seen it before? Then he remembered. This was the band on the poster in his room, the poster Maud had put on the wall to make him feel at home. And they weren't playing instruments at all. They were starting huge chain saws! The man who would have been the drummer was operating a circular saw with five or six blades where the drum heads should have been.

Then Eli saw that it wasn't a band, didn't even look like a band. It was just five guys in plaid shirts and red suspenders, with silver hard hats and sturdy-looking boots. They began to lop off trees right and left. The trees fell into neat stacks, like the one he was making at home out of the firewood. They were singing as they worked; it was the song the monkey guards sang as they patrolled the castle in *The Wizard of Oz*. ''Woah-hee-oh Ee-oh-oh.'' Right behind them came a bulldozer on tracks with a blade ten feet tall, spewing black smoke out of tall chrome smokestacks. The blade leveled the ground and tore out the plants and shrubs left by the cutters. Other machines worked behind the bulldozer paving and painting so that, as the machines went by, they left a perfectly flat parking lot, with yellow lines to show where the cars should park.

In one of the parking spaces was the little Honda dirt bike. Eli ran to it and tried to start it. He kicked and kicked but nothing happened. He looked carefully and saw that it was a bicycle, an old green bike with fat tires and a tank. He began to pedal for the farm. He wanted to get help. The bicycle moved ridiculously slowly, like in a cartoon. Hardly moving at all. From time to time, the cutters passed beside him, with the machines roaring behind them, laying their strip of parking lot. Frank glared at Eli with his steely blue eyes and smiled that cold smile. Once Eli saw him mouth the word *faggot*, and the other cutters laughed. On the bicycle, it was as though he was standing still and the cutters and Frank and the machines and the road were all floating lazily past him. Eli thought it was like the way they made those old-fashioned movies, where the people and the car remained still and flat scenes of streets moved behind them.

He jumped off the bike, let it fall, and began to run. After what seemed like hours he arrived at the farmhouse, covered with sweat and completely exhausted. It was dark; Maud and Danny were asleep. Eli burst into their room and began yelling for help, telling them all at once that his trees were being cut down and about Frank and the machines and the parking lot and Styletto and everything else.

Maud got out of bed and went to the closet to put on her coat. Eli was amazed to see that she could walk. There were no crutches anywhere in the room. Maud looked younger and not so tired in the dim light of the bedside lamp. She told Eli she would come with him to talk to the cutters, see what she could do. Danny, though, did not get out of bed. "Maud," he said, "don't bother those boys. They're just trying to make a living, they gotta eat don't they? You just stay here," Danny told her. "You aren't going anywhere tonight."

Eli was surprised to hear Danny talk that way, he was usually so kind and soft-spoken. Maud glanced sideways at Eli, rolled her eyes skyward, then removed the coat and crawled back into bed.

He didn't know what to do. Danny rolled over and went back to sleep. Maud gave Eli a very sad look and turned off the lamp. He stood at the foot of the bed feeling strange and helpless.

Outside the bedroom window a nearly full moon was just coming up over the field. Far off, Eli heard the deep *who-whoo* of a great horned owl. A tear formed, waited at the corner of Eli's right eye, then rolled slowly down his cheek. He did not move to brush it off as it gently left its salt taste on his lower lip, slid to the bottom of his chin, then dropped into the darkness.

Eli looked again at the shape that was Danny and Maud asleep in the moonlight, then turned and went back to bed.

The long, lazy days of August passed, one by one, relentlessly. All over the Willamette Valley, corn grew taller than a man and then sprouted silky ears. What had been white blossoms in July were now hard green berries the size of the end of your little finger on every blackberry thicket on every creek and ditch in every part of the valley. The days grew shorter and there was always a feeling of autumn early in the morning, yet the sun poured down on the valley, turning the hay-fields to a golden brown and drying up shallow water.

Maud watched Eli at his work. She marveled at the change in him. The mountain of wood which was to be their winter heat had dwindled slowly, then disappeared, under Eli's splitting maul. The garden flourished with his care. He mended the fences, mowed the lawn, even kept the old milk cow fat and sassy.

She saw a different person now that summer was coming to an end, somehow changed from the cocky city boy who had arrived in June. Eli was more muscled now after weeks of hard work, and deeply tanned. He moved with more confidence. He seemed to trust his body to do what he wanted it to do. Gone were the tight stone-washed jeans and the lizard-skin boots, gone were the sunglasses, even the diamond stud spent most of its time on the table in his room. Eli chose to wear a simple uniform now of Levis, work boots, and a T-shirt, topped off with a farmer's cap, which served to keep his long blond hair out of his face.

Along with the change in his appearance came a change in attitude. Eli seemed cheerful most of the time. He didn't seem to mind the lack of television anymore and he managed to keep busy. He's always hungry, Maud thought. The loud, harsh chords of the Strato-caster could be heard less often now in the evenings. They were replaced by the mellower sound of the old Guild acoustic guitar that Danny had given Eli.

And the songs had changed. Maud couldn't put her finger on exactly how they were different. They were all loud. But somehow, Eli's songs, as they came through the bedroom wall, had grown more complex, more thoughtful. He seemed to be trying to put more into them. She was learning to like them.

The work had begun on the trees up the road. Every day pickup trucks and machinery went past the farm, and Maud watched Eli stop what he was doing and follow them with his eyes. Sometimes he got a faraway look and she knew he was thinking of the special place he had found in the forest. Often he would get on the dirt bike and ride away and Maud knew where he went.

But he never said a word to her or to Danny. Whatever feelings he had about the logging he kept to himself.

Dear Rick,

How is the tour? I got the clippings a few days ago. Thanks. I'll put them in my scrapbook with the others. It sounds like you guys are doing great. Way to go! And thanks for the new T-shirts. It's real hot here. Danny says it's a dry year. I split all the wood! Maud says I look like a macho man now with my big muscles. I guess she is teasing me. I've written a few good songs lately. Danny and I made a tape of three of them and I want you to hear it. Mostly I work outside in the garden and the yard. I'm learning to enjoy helping. I guess it makes me feel like I'm part of the family here. I don't feel like I'm sponging off Maud and Danny now. It seemed like every time I used to go to Moffett with Danny, somebody would give me a raft about my hair or my earring or something. Lately I have just been staying here. I guess I like that the best. That way I don't get into trouble. They are going to cut down a bunch of gigantic trees a couple of miles up the road from here. It's a place I used to like to go to think. Some old guy named Simpson owns the trees and just decided to cut them down! It makes me real mad but Danny says there's nothing we can do about it. I've been up there a lot and it's real ugly! They are cut-

ting down a few trees right now to make a road.
Everything is brown and dead where they cut them.
After they make the road in, Danny says they'll just
mow down everything and haul it away. I wish
there was something I could do to stop it.
Thanks again for the package.

Love,
Eli

After his work was done in the morning, Eli would ride the dirt bike up to the logging site. At first he had decided to stay away completely. He wanted to remember it as it was. But he could hear the sound of the bulldozers and trucks when the wind was right and finally his curiosity was too much for him and he began to ride up there.

The place they had begun to work was some distance from the place he called Eli's trees. They were making a road in, starting at the corner of the area marked with red ribbons. Yet Eli knew it was only a matter of time. He watched as the fallers cut the trees and the crane stacked them in piles, like Tinkertoys. He saw the big yellow Caterpillars push down what was left and level the soil. Then came the dump trucks, dumping hundreds of loads of rock to make the road. Slowly and noisily the road snaked its way into the forest, getting ready to carry out the logs.

The workers quit in the middle of the afternoon, and

several times Eli had waited until they had all shot down the road in their dusty pickups, then walked around to see what they had done. He was surprised at how little road they had completed, they didn't seem to be getting very far into the forest. For all the noise and dust, these men had done surprisingly little damage so far.

One day, a Sunday, Eli rode up to the logging site and walked to the end of the rock road. It now wound several hundred yards into the woods and stopped at the base of the biggest tree Eli had seen yet. Eli sat with his back against the tree and thought. He looked around and saw that to his right was the creek down in a ravine. He could hear it pouring over the rocks down there. To his left was a steep slope, covered with boulders and vine maple turning yellow. From time to time he tipped his head back and looked straight up into the big fir. He could see the branches flow out of the trunk and sweep down toward the earth. He could hear the wind sing in the green needles. He felt dizzy as he watched the top, far above him, sway against the dark blue sky.

Eli saw all of this. He saw in his mind the dream and Frank smiling coldly as he paved the forest. He felt the strong hands on his shoulders, pushing him to the bottom of the silent, green water; he shivered as he remembered the black emptiness of near-death.

Eli remembered waking up to the quiet music of a morning in the trees, remembered being alive and whole. He recalled the taunts and remarks that came from so many of the people in Moffett.

For some reason he thought of Maud and her quiet determination, her strength.

And then something just went *click*. It wasn't as though Eli changed, it wasn't that he learned anything new. Somehow he simply got to a certain point in his mind and he knew, he was positive, there was no going back.

He returned to the farm. Maud and Danny were still away in town. He found four six-foot two-by-fours inside the barn. Next he looked around until he found a roll of rope in Danny's toolshed. He put this with the boards. Then he went into the house and emptied out his backpack on the bed. Next he found bread and fruit, some peanuts, and some blackberry jam in the kitchen and put these into the pack. He filled two plastic jugs with water and put those into the pack also. He fastened his sleeping bag to its place on the frame of the backpack. At the last minute, he ran back into the house and got his notebook and a pen and added these to the food and water.

It took two trips to get the boards and the rope to the logging site, and before he left on the third trip, with the backpack, he wrote a short note to Maud and Danny, telling them he had decided to camp in the woods. They would think that was a little strange, but at least they wouldn't worry too much.

When Eli arrived at the end of the logging road with the pack, he stopped for a minute to gather his thoughts and see if he had forgotten anything. Then he looked around until he found a good-sized rock and tied one end of the rope to it.

Most big Douglas firs don't have living branches except at the top. Fortunately for Eli, this tree had thick, strong limbs along most of its height. Even so, it took eight tries before he succeeded in putting the rock over the lowest branch. Slowly he fed more rope until the rock dangled before his nose. He untied the rock and quickly made a slip knot, then pulled until the sturdy rope was securely fastened to the branch, forty feet above him.

Eli used the pocketknife Danny had given him to cut a ten-foot length from the end of the rope. He tied it around his waist before tying the boards and the pack onto the rope hanging from the tree, spacing them about fifteen feet apart.

Because the rope was so thin, it was much more difficult to climb than the one he had known in gym class last year. Eli had not counted on that. But by gripping hard and using his legs to help him, he was soon sitting on the branch, looking at the boards and his blue nylon backpack below.

The first thing Eli did was use the piece of rope he had wrapped around his waist to tie himself to a branch right above his head; he knew that a fall meant certain death. After he was secured to the tree, he began to pull up the two-by-fours. Slowly they swung up to him, one at a time, until he had them all. Then up came the backpack and the rest of the rope.

Eli used pieces of the rope to tie the two-by-fours across two big branches so that he had a kind of platform he could sit on. He arranged his sleeping bag and his pack on this narrow ledge, dangled his legs out into space, helped himself to some bread and some of Maud's delicious jam, and began the long vigil.

9

Like a bird
You sit in a tree
The days go by
You're wild and free

You would live here forever
If there was a way
If you could fly
You'd just sail away

Eli couldn't have climbed a more troublesome tree. He didn't know this as he dozed on the narrow platform that had become his home for the night. Oh, he knew there was bound to be some commotion in the morning when the workers found him there. Some serious commotion. Of that Eli was certain.

But what he could not know was this: The giant fir in which he waited was located at the exact meeting place of a massive escarpment of basalt and his creek. Put another way: There was nowhere for the road to go but through the tree in which Eli slept. To the left was the creek, burbling in its canyon. To the right, the rocky hillside climbed steeply away. Just beyond the big tree, the escarpment veered to the north and leveled out; the creek made a sharp turn to the south. The land opened up into a broad, flat forest. This was the Simpson land that was to be cut.

It was as though the broad forest land was a vast bottle that narrowed to a tiny opening. And Eli's tree was the cork. Eli had roosted in the most important tree in Mr. Simpson's whole logging operation.

When the first workers arrived at 5:30 the next morning, there he sat, huddled in his sleeping bag, legs dangling over the edge of his little home.

Waiting.

Eli had been a bit worried during the night that some tree cutter would rush out of his pickup and begin to saw down the tree before he knew Eli was there. At first light he had gathered an armful of the dead branches that grew out of the trunk near his platform. These were brittle and easily broken. He was prepared to drop a branch or two on some guy's head if need be, to get his attention. He certainly didn't want the tree to fall over with him still in it.

But it didn't happen that way.

A big four-wheel-drive pickup rolled in and stopped

several hundred yards from the tree. Two men got out and gathered together their equipment from the back of the truck. They were wearing silver hard hats. Eli watched them walk slowly from the truck, the metal spikes on the soles of their boots making a harsh rasp against the new rock of the road. They were discussing their weekend, Eli could hear every word they said.

When they got directly under him, the men put down their saws, oilcan, and canvas tool bag. They leaned against the tree to have a cigarette and some coffee from a thermos. Eli could smell the acrid smoke as it rose from their resting place below.

When they finished smoking, the two men began a careful search of the area, as loggers always do before they begin cutting. They were looking for anything that might hang up a falling tree or cause one to roll strangely when it hit the ground. They were looking for the best place for the tree to fall. They were checking to see how soft the ground was near the creekbank. They were looking for dead branches, called widow-makers, which can fall out of a tree onto the worker below.

That was when one of the men spotted Eli.

"What the hell—! Hey, Willy, lookathis! Hey, kid, what in the hell are you doin' up there? Holy smoke, I never! Willy!"

The man was totally confused. He was shouting for his partner and shouting at Eli at the same time. Making little short runs away, as if to go get Willy, then coming back, his eyes never leaving Eli's perch high in the big tree.

"Willy!"

Willy had been off some distance into the forest but he came on the run and joined the first man in standing and staring up at Eli.

"Hey, kid, you can't camp here! What in the devil made you climb this tree?"

Eli sat quietly, waiting, not making a sound.

"I'm talking to you, boy, girl, whatever you are. Get down outta that tree!"

Silence.

"Willy, it don't say much. Have you ever seen such a thing? Is it a girl? How the hell did she get up there anyway?"

A quick look of recognition came into Willy's face and a brief smile flashed across his mouth. Eli recognized Willy as one of the men who had been with Frank at the river that day: dark hair, blue eyes, big nose.

"That ain't no girl, Joe. I seen this kid before. Someone told me he's up here from California, staying down the road there with Danny Connolly. He musta got bored and decided to build hisself a little tree house.

"Hey, boy! You got yourself a mighty high tree house. You're going to have to get out of it, though, 'cause this here tree belongs to us. You picked a real bad place to have fun, you mighta hurt yourself."

94

Willy was trying to be reasonable. Pretending.

"Come on down now, kid, we're ready to go to work."

Still no answer from Eli. He was still waiting.

"Willy, I think the kid must be deaf or something. He don't look like he hears a word we're saying."

"He hears us, Joe. Like I told you, I seen this kid before. He thinks he's Mr. California Smartypants.

"Hey, Mr. California Smartypants!" Willy, with his hands cupped, yelled up at Eli. "There ain't nobody here to save your butt today is there? Maybe we'll just cut you outta this tree. Maybe we can grab a little of that faggot hair as you go by."

Willy got a big kick out of himself at this. He laughed loudly, then picked up his saw. Still laughing, he adjusted the saw, got it ready to run. Wrapped his fingers around the starting rope.

"Okay, longhair. What's it gonna be? You gonna come outta that tree the way you went up or you gonna come down the hard way?"

Eli's moment had come. Before Willy could start the saw Eli threw off the sleeping bag and stood on the edge of the platform, like on a diving board. Holding a three-foot piece of branch, thick as a man's arm, jagged on both ends, in front of him, directly over the men's heads, he said, "Maybe you're bluffing, redneck, maybe not. But if you get that saw into this tree, this hunk of wood may just slip out of my hands and drop you like

95

a piece of dead meat. And I have some more up here in case I miss." Eli had been practicing this little speech all morning, just in case he needed it.

A tree faller has a morbid fear of something falling out of a tree and hitting him. Eli expected that he could outbluff a tree cutter with his piece of branch but he did not expect the two men to react the way they did. They sprang back away from the tree and scrambled to safety, abandoning the saws and other equipment. They acted as if they'd seen a ghost.

"I can't believe it," Joe sputtered, "that kid is crazier than hell! What's he trying to do, kill us or something?"

"Listen, Joe, I think we better talk to the boss. Call the police. I don't know what this kid is up to but I don't like it. I don't even want to mess with it. Let's get out of here."

After about an hour, Joe and Willy came again, with their boss and another man, who turned out to be Frank. Willy had dug him up somewhere and he didn't want to miss the fun. All four men stayed a respectable distance from the base of the tree. Evidently none of them wanted to find out if Eli would really drop a branch on them.

The logging boss was a well spoken man in slacks and a sports shirt and shiny shoes. His hair was short and graying at the temples below the silver hard hat. He was a man who seemed to know how to work with people. He reminded Eli of a math teacher he had last year.

This man spoke in a friendly way and Eli found himself explaining why he had climbed the tree; telling the boss that he did not want them to cut his trees. The man patiently explained that the trees and the land belonged to Mr. Simpson and that he had decided to have them cut while the price of lumber was high. "There is nothing any of us can or should do about that," he explained calmly. "There are many other beautiful places for you to enjoy. You are costing me hundreds of dollars an hour keeping my men from doing their job."

It took a while for Eli to convince the boss that he wasn't going to come down, but he finally managed to do so and all four men drove away. Frank looked disappointed as he turned toward the truck to leave.

Soon the boss arrived again, this time in his shiny new pickup. Another man was with him, a man with climbing gear. As the climber strapped the spikes to his boots and attached the harness around his shoulders and waist, the boss spoke again to Eli.

"Son, we're going to have to remove you from this tree. I'm sorry. I know you love this forest. I love it as well. But climbing a tree is not going to help you get what you want; you have no right to be here.

"Now I know you won't throw that piece of wood down on my man. I'm afraid that would be assault and you'd go to jail. If you killed old George there, why, that would be murder, wouldn't it? You don't really want to hurt anyone, I know that. Why don't you just toss that piece of wood down, now, way over there somewhere, so nobody gets hurt. Okay?''

The boss was talking in calm, reasonable tones, being careful not to say anything that might cause Eli to do anything rash. Eli could tell that the boss was trying extremely hard to remain calm and soft-spoken.

He could also tell that the boss thought he was crazier than a loon.

Just then more visitors arrived.

A tan-and-brown pickup pulled up behind the boss and two uniformed deputy sheriffs got out. It made Eli's stomach tighten into a ball to see that the deputy on the passenger side brought a shotgun with him and held it loosely at his side. They also had a dog. The deputies were wearing mirror shades and baseball-type caps and looked like they meant business.

Behind the police car came a dirty Toyota. It was Maud. She gathered her crutches from the backseat and began to swing her way toward the tree. The deputy with the shotgun held out his arm to block her path as she came up behind him. He didn't speak and didn't turn to look at Maud, just held out his arm. She stopped and looked up at Eli in the tree.

George had begun to climb the tree. He had a cable that ran around the tree and hooked to his harness. He would take a few steps, with the metal spikes on his boots digging into the bark of the tree, then raise up the cable, leaning out into space to hold himself from falling. Then a few more steps, then raise the cable. Slowly he was making his way to Eli's platform. Eli knew that the threat of a dropped branch would not slow him. He'd have to think of something else. Quick.

"Now George isn't going to hurt you," the boss was saying in his teacher voice. "He's going to come up to your tree house and then lower you down carefully with a rope. If you'll be calm and careful, no one will get hurt. Then you can go home and we'll forget the whole thing, okay?"

The deputies had moved up to where the boss was standing. They were talking quietly to one another. The climber was now around to the side, getting closer. Eli could no longer see him, but he could hear the regular rasp of the cable and the measured sound of the spikes sinking into the bark. He could hear the man's breathing.

Quickly, Eli untied the rope from around his waist. For some reason, he took off his shirt and tossed it on top of his backpack. He pulled off his boots and socks. Then he stood up and stepped to the very edge of the platform, wearing nothing but his jeans, curling his toes over like a diver, extending his arms like a bird. He saw the boss give a signal with his hand and he heard the climber stop.

A look of surprise had come over the boss's face. One of the cops took off his sunglasses and stared up at Eli with an open mouth. He saw the look of terror in Maud's eyes. She seemed to be frozen where she stood, leaning into the crutches.

Eli did not know where the words came from that he heard himself speaking—there, balancing high above the forest floor, the wind in his hair, the big tree swaying gently, his arms outstretched as though he were going to take flight:

"This is my forest and you cannot have it," he said to the people who stared silently up at him. "I will leave it when I choose to leave. If you try to take me away, I will leave my forest like an eagle. I will fly. You cannot stop me from flying away."

With this, Eli leaned even farther forward and bent his knees, shook his hair from his eyes, ready for flight. What had started as another bluff had now become something else. Eli saw the ground sway gently beneath him. He saw the long cut of the road through the forest stretch out before him; an avenue for flight. Eli felt the wind against his bare chest, remembered his flight into the green river, felt the earth curving away from him, endlessly. He did not know what he would do if the man below him continued his climb.

Even the boss knew he couldn't deal with boys who flew. The climber went down the tree the same way he had come up and he and the boss returned to town. Eli heard the boss say, as they walked to the pickup, "Well, he can't stay up there forever."

Eli resumed his sitting position on the platform. He

did not know what had made him threaten to fly out of the tree, but it had stopped the climber from removing him and he was not unhappy about what he had done.

The police retreated some distance down the logging road and sat in their truck. Eli could hear the endless chatter of their two-way radio.

Maud made her way slowly, carefully, to the base of the tree. She looked up at Eli. Everything was in her eyes.

"Eli," she said, "you be careful up there."

That was all she said. Then she turned around and went home.

Many things happened to surprise Eli as he sat patiently in his tree. One thing, of course, was the fact that he had chosen to climb the one tree that could shut down the entire logging operation. They could not go around him and there was no other way into the area they wanted to cut. This fact pleased Eli immensely.

It had been quite a surprise to him when the boss had sent a climber to fetch him from his perch. Somehow, Eli had expected the loggers to threaten him with cutting the tree, but he had never thought they might climb up to him.

The third big surprise was his own reaction to the climber. It had not been planned; he had not known what he was going to do until he found himself standing on the brink of death, threatening to jump, speaking in a voice he did not know he possessed. Now as he sat alone with the wind, he thought of a word and it made him shudder. *Suicide.* The chills came whenever he found himself staring at that word, that thought.

Had he really meant to jump? Would he have flown out over the people who had stood below, to land crumpled and dead at their feet? Eli didn't know. He knew that it had started with a threat, something to scare away the climber.

Once he had been walking home from school with a couple of guys, and two older kids came out of nowhere and began to harass him. Calling him names, making crude jokes about his mother. It happened that Eli had in his backpack that day a steel knife he had made in metal shop. He whipped out the knife, growled fiercely at the older kids, took a stance as though he meant business, and threatened to kill both of them. A bluff. The teenagers hurried off. Eli and his friends got a big kick out of the whole thing. He had never intended to hurt anybody.

And this threat, to fly out of a tree, was this like that, just a bluff? He thought it was. All the same, sitting safely on his platform, his rope back around his waist, Eli felt pretty shaky when he remembered how his toes had curled over the edge of the rough two-by-four and his body had hung precariously out into empty space.

Eli had about come to grips with what he had done and why he had done it and had eaten a little bread and jam when the next big surprise arrived. The news media had gotten wind of a boy who thought he was an eagle, a boy with long blond hair who lived high in a massive fir tree, a boy who was holding off an entire logging operation single-handedly.

Eli, it seemed, was about to become famous.

10

The people come to see you fall
They only point and stare
They giggle and they whisper
So you know that they don't care

When the right one comes, the one you trust
You'll know it right away
Her words are music in your ears
You'll be back on earth today

Well, maybe not famous, exactly. After all of the film crews had taken endless pictures, after all the serious, well dressed reporters had yelled question after question up to Eli and written down the answers in little notebooks and recorded them on tape, after all of the dust and commotion and noise of the newspaper and television people from Portland, Salem, and Eugene had settled, after all of this, the story of Eli and his trees turned out to be a very short story on the evening news and a small article in the back sections of several newspapers.

Mostly, people either didn't see the story or didn't care.

But the people of Moffett noticed.

Little towns like Moffett don't get too much news coverage. The last time the television stations had mentioned the town was two years before when a log truck had overturned, blocking the road completely for nearly twenty-four hours. Now, there was this long-haired kid perched in a tree telling the cameras that he didn't think it was right that the trees should be cut. Some kind of environmentalist nut, probably. Said he was from California. Some crazy kid living in a tree, and right there outside of Moffett.

Many of the townspeople thought it was downright embarrassing. And they came in droves to see this sight for themselves.

Some of them giggled and pointed and then left. Some of them stared for a while, shook their heads, and left. Quite a few talked to Eli, asked him why he was up there. He always told them he was there to save his trees. They mostly told him he shouldn't be getting in the way of progress; a lot of folks said they hoped he went to jail.

Eli could see they all thought he was crazy.

Danny and Maud came by in the evening. They hadn't seen him on television of course, but they had seen the paper. Maud had cut out the story, and she read it to Eli as he sat with his legs dangling over the edge of his tree house. It sounded funny to hear about himself in the newspaper like that. He hadn't really thought this was such a big deal. The reporter had made the story seem important, somehow:

BOY CLIMBS TREE TO SAVE FOREST

Twelve-year-old Eli James Connolly says that the reason he refuses to climb out of his tree is that he intends to keep loggers from entering a forest he has come to love. Eli, who is staying with his aunt and uncle for the summer near Moffett, has been in the tree since Sunday afternoon. Eli claims to have enough food and water to last for "weeks" in his perch, which is about forty feet from the ground. It seems that the logging slated for this area has been completely halted because the boy refuses to leave the tree. Climbers have been unable to remove him. The logging foreman, Sam Jones, says that he is unhappy about the situation but does not wish to endanger the boy's life. Jones says that he intends to wait until Eli comes down on his own and then proceed with the logging operation. "He can't stay up there forever," Jones said.

Danny and Maud did not try to talk Eli into coming down. If they had thought about doing so at one time, they had now changed their minds. It was clear to them that Eli had made a decision. Eli almost felt that both of them were proud of him. He couldn't be sure.

They did seem a little worried he would fall, but Eli showed them his safety rope and that seemed to reassure both of them. If Maud had told Danny about the incident earlier, about Eli threatening to fly off the platform, he showed no sign. Eli guessed she hadn't told him.

They wanted to know, of course, when he thought he was coming down. It had been easy to give a flip answer to the strangers who had asked him that question. "I'll come down when they promise not to cut the trees and not before." That's what he had told the reporters.

But he could see the real concern on both Danny's and Maud's face as they craned their necks to look up at him.

"When are you coming home?" they wanted to know.

"In a few days." He heard himself telling Danny and Maud he would not make it more than a few days.

Eli suddenly felt very tired.

* * *

By Wednesday morning, the flood of curious people had turned into a trickle. Eli's food and water were about gone and he was weary of sitting. A reporter from the local weekly newspaper came to get his story and Eli refused to talk to him. The questions were always the same; he was sick of them.

Maud came to talk to him every morning and both she and Danny came in the evening. They always asked if there was anything they could do, anything they could bring. Eli always said no.

Old man Simpson had two men watching the tree at all times, day and night. Their standing orders were these: If the kid comes down, grab the kid, cut down the tree, and call the police. He was taking no chances.

These men sat in their pickup mostly, playing cards, listening to a country-western station, looking at magazines. They talked and laughed most of the time. They could afford to laugh. The men were getting paid their regular wages to baby-sit a hippie kid in a tree house, as they put it. One guy that came in the evenings always brought a pistol. He used it to shoot squirrels, lizards, birds—anything that moved. Once the man laughed to his friend that he ought to just "blow the little faggot out of his nest," and waved the pistol lazily in Eli's direction. The friend laughed, too, but said, "Naw, then we'd have to go to work." They both got a big kick out of this.

108

Sometime before noon—Eli didn't have a watch—a big, red Ford sedan pulled slowly up behind the pickup and stopped. Eli could see a woman with short dark hair behind the wheel. Unlike the others who had come, who had jumped out of their cars almost before they stopped rolling, this woman remained in her car. She seemed to be organizing some papers, going through her briefcase. She put on her glasses. She took them off. She shuffled through some more folders. Eli wondered if she was going to get out of the Ford at all. He wondered if she was a police officer.

Finally the door opened and she stepped out. Eli watched as she put on her blazer, then checked her hair quickly in her reflection in the window. Then she picked up the brown briefcase and walked quickly to the driver's side of the dusty pickup.

Eli could hear the authority and the businesslike tone in her voice. He could not hear the words. She spoke briefly to Simpson's men, then handed them a manila folder through the window. They seemed unhappy about what she told them, and the man on the passenger side of the truck tried to argue with her. The dark-haired woman answered sternly, then opened her briefcase and fished out a piece of paper, which she held up for them to see but did not give them. She returned the paper to her briefcase. The driver picked up his telephone, said something in a gruff voice, then waited. Finally someone came on the other end and the man asked a few questions.

Then an amazing thing happened. The man slammed down the phone, started up the truck, turned it around, and roared off down the road in a shower of gravel and dust. Eli was left alone in his tree for the first time.

Alone, that is, except for the woman.

She walked quickly, carrying her briefcase in her left hand, until she was directly under Eli.

"You are, I presume, Eli Connolly?" she asked in a firm, deep voice. This was the voice of someone who was in complete control, who knew exactly what she was doing. This was a voice you could trust. Eli answered that, yes, he was Eli Connolly.

"Eli, I am Diane Gooden. I am a partner in the firm of Flynt, Weiser, Gooden, and Marsh. It is my understanding that you are opposed to the clear-cut logging which is scheduled to take place here and that is why you have climbed this tree. Is that correct?" Diane Gooden was shading her eyes with her right hand and looking up at Eli.

"I love these trees and I don't think they should cut them," he answered. It seemed like a feeble answer; Eli felt inadequate talking to this lady. She seemed to be able to see right through him. She could read minds for all Eli knew.

"Eli, I have taken a personal interest in this situation. I have my own reasons for doing so. Perhaps we could talk about that sometime. In any case, after talking with your aunt Maud yesterday and doing a bit of research on my own, I appeared before Judge Widmore in Salem this morning and he has issued this." The dark-haired woman opened her briefcase, still holding it in her left hand, and pulled out a sheaf of paper. "A restraining order which temporarily halts any logging in this watershed. I thought you'd like to know."

"Does that mean Simpson can't cut down my trees?" Eli asked, not sure exactly what the woman had just told him.

"It means he cannot cut them for now. We will have to go to court to stop him permanently from cutting them. I'm sure Judge Widmore would be very interested in what you have to say about, um, your trees. That is, if you feel like you might want to come down from your home up there."

Eli saw her smile, then become serious once again.

"Well, Eli, I'll leave this copy of the court order right here." She placed the sheaf of papers on the ground at her feet. "You may look at it at your leisure. You will be interested to know that no charges will be pressed against you. You are free to come down when you like. I'm sure your aunt and uncle will be more than glad to see you again."

Again, the smile.

"I'm leaving my card. Call me if you are interested in speaking to the judge."

The woman turned to go. Then she stopped and turned back to face Eli. Her voice had changed, become more gentle, caring, softer. Diane Gooden was now talking like a mother.

"Eli, I have a boy about your age at home. Please be careful getting down out of that tree. Okay?"

Then she was getting into her Ford, and then she was gone.

Sitting alone in his tree, hearing Diane Gooden's words again and again in his mind, Eli was very surprised to find himself thinking about his mother.

It had been so long since he had seen her. Pam—tall, blond, a model. Eli remembered that she was always waiting for her next assignment, waiting for the phone to ring. Magazines stacked around the apartment, magazines with pictures of his mother in them, on the covers.

Somehow when he thought of her now, Eli always remembered his mother as poised on the sofa, pale against the black vinyl, her short platinum hair like a light around her face. Poised, like she was waiting, looking off into space, way off, her cigarette sending blue smoke curling around her face. Endlessly swirling the ice in her drink. Swirling, swirling the glass around, the glass of Chivas, always turning the glass, clinking the ice.

It was odd to think of her now, odd that he should remember Pam so vividly at this moment when he had so many things to think about. He wondered what she would think if she could see him here, tied to a Douglas fir tree in Oregon.

112

He smiled. It would be impossible for her to imagine such a thing, and somehow it made Eli feel better to know that.

After a long time, the birds began to sing again. The August afternoon was still and the creek bubbled around and over the rocks. A squirrel was cutting cones from a hemlock tree, getting ready for the winter, dropping them in a shower onto the logging road below. It chattered noisily as it worked, not wanting to lose even a single cone to any intruder. A red-headed snake stretched in the shade of a rock at the edge of the road.

Eli heard and saw all of this. He sat, with his legs over the side of his platform, savoring the feeling that he could come down whenever he liked. He was in no hurry.

He tried to think about everything that had happened since Sunday when he had climbed up into this tree. Somehow it had all become jumbled up in his mind. Everything ran together. He could not remember each separate thing that had happened. He couldn't even remember what exactly had caused him to climb up here, it seemed like so long ago.

Instead, he remembered how he had felt, how everything had seemed to him, like a collage of many colors.

Eli thought about the anger of the workers who had found him here. He saw their faces, so much like Frank's face, masks of hatred. He thought about the cool control of the boss, but remembered how he had slammed the door of his shiny truck and spun the tires when he was forced to leave without getting Eli out of the tree.

He saw the faces of the reporters and heard their questions, over and over again; saw that they didn't care about him or what he had to say, or why; saw that these people only cared about themselves.

More than anything, Eli felt the warmth of Danny and Maud. The warmth of their understanding and caring, of not treating him as though he was just some stupid kid up in a tree. The warmth of trust.

He let all of this happen in his head for as long as it wanted to.

Then he dropped his backpack to the ground, lowered the two-by-fours the same way he had raised them, slid down the rope, and picked up the thick packet of papers Diane Gooden had brought him. He left everything else—even the Honda—where it lay, for Danny to pick up later, and headed for home.

Walking.

One foot at a time, step by step, on the good, green earth.

11

Dreaming, over and over
Of falling, of flying,
Of dancing wildly
Through space, whirling
Into darkness. Dreaming
Of the earth rushing up,
Then turning to water,
Dark green water
Tearing at your throat,
Holding you, crushing you.
Dreaming of the eerie silence
Of death,
Then waking into the world
Again, seeing the light
And knowing you are here.

Late summer came to the Willamette Valley with cool, misty mornings and hot, hazy afternoons. Leaves began to show yellow here and there on the hawthorne trees at the end of the driveway. Tomatoes reddened and peaches turned gold. Some nights a fire crackled in the Fisher stove.

Eli's nightmares about falling, always falling into darkness, had almost stopped. Once in a while, though, he would awaken, shaking, covered with sweat, tears in his eyes. He would know he had been screaming. When the dreams had first begun, either Danny or Maud would rush to his bedside to comfort him, awakened by Eli's screams of terror in the night. Now they remained in bed, knowing there was nothing to be done but wait. They were glad the dreams came less frequently.

One morning in early September Eli awoke to the sound of the alarm clock, showered, pulled on his STYLETTO SUMMER TOUR T-shirt, faded Levis, and Converse All-Stars, and went into the kitchen for breakfast. Maud was there, waiting for him. The smell of buttermilk pancakes on the hot black griddle filled the room. Warm blackberry syrup simmered on the back of the stove.

"Well," she asked, her eyes sparkling, "what do you think? Are you ready for this?"

Today was the first day of school. Eli was a great deal more nervous than he wanted anyone to think, even Maud. She and Danny had talked with him about what to expect, about some of the kids who would be in his class, about some of the big differences between Moffett Elementary School and Fairfield Middle School, where he had gone last year. They had warned him that the teachers probably wouldn't put up with much goofing around, especially from a new boy who looked like Eli looked, and that the old bus driver wouldn't wait for him if he was late.

Now he glanced out the window, half expecting to see the bus, and picked at his breakfast. "Yeah, I guess," he replied absently, his mind on the bus ride, the school, the teachers. Eli saw Maud stop spooning batter onto the griddle, ladle poised in midair, and look at him. Her gray eyes narrowed with concern. Before she could say anything, Eli forced himself to jazz up his answer, so Maud wouldn't worry about him.

"Hey, this is going to be a piece of cake," he said, sitting up a little straighter in the chair. "I'll probably be running the place by Friday."

Maud smiled, went back to making pancakes. Eli was working on his timing, timing was his specialty. He waited—one, two, three.

"And when I am in charge, the first thing I'll do is make summer vacation a month longer." They both laughed.

The bus ride was long and noisy. Kids stared and pointed, whispered to each other and giggled. At the school there was more staring and giggling. It was not only because he looked different, Eli knew, that he was the center of attention at Moffett Elementary School. He was the famous tree climber and everyone had seen him on TV.

And with only nineteen students in the entire seventh grade it was hard to hide.

So Eli told jokes at recess. He did card tricks. As the days passed, he let it be known that he was a guitar player and a songwriter. When someone recognized the name on his T-shirt, he very casually mentioned that Styletto was his dad's band. He talked to the girls.

117

By the end of the first week the giggling and whispering had stopped. There were three boys whose fathers had lost some work because of Eli's "tree house" as they called it, and these three hated Eli passionately, although they never challenged him. Some of the other kids seemed to grant him a grudging respect, without having much to do with him. Most of Eli's classmates, however, liked him. A few even showed admiration for him.

One day, for fun, Eli wore his diamond earring, his lizard-skin boots, and everything else that went with his L.A. "look": the belt, the rings, the shades, the headband. It was too much. Even Amy, a girl in his class who seemed more willing than anyone else to accept Eli for what he was, told him he looked weird. She said, "Eli, you look crazy." Eli looked in the mirror and felt pretty ridiculous. He took off the jewelry and put it with the sunglasses in his desk. He traded the boots for his P.E. shoes. He went to find Amy.

"What an improvement, huh? What do you think of me without my Halloween costume?" Eli grinned, held out his arms, spun around. He waited for her reaction.

"You know," she told him, completely ignoring his change in appearance, "you really remind me of Sting. Your eyes are like his and there's something about the way you both look so *serious* all the time."

Serious. Eli didn't get it. He didn't know anything about Sting and he certainly didn't think of himself as serious. He thought he was pretty funny.

"No," Amy went on, scrutinizing Eli's face, "not serious, intense; you and Sting are both so *intense*. And you both have those pointed nostrils. I love pointed nostrils."

Eli was amazed. He never thought she had looked at his nostrils!

"Well, anyway—" she said, then stopped. Eli was still trying to remember what his nostrils looked like. Amy started again. "You know, sometimes Sting—he has blond hair kind of like yours, you know—sometimes he has long hair and sometimes he cuts it off. It's short now, I saw him on TV a couple of nights ago. He is *so* cool. You know, maybe you should cut your hair. I mean, I like it and everything, but I think you'd look just like him—Sting, I mean—if you had shorter hair. Cool. You know what I mean?"

Just then two of Amy's friends came by and she said, "See ya," and left Eli alone, leaning against a brick wall, studying a long lock of his hair, trying to recall what Sting looked like.

He thought about what Amy had said, thought about change, about fitting in.

Then Rick called one Saturday afternoon to say that Styletto was to go into a studio in Toronto soon to cut a new album. This album would have a different sound, a harder edge, than anything Styletto had done in the past. Rick explained to Eli that, after playing with some of the world's greatest bands on this tour, he realized it was time to change, time for something different. He sounded excited. The album would be sold only in Canada and a tour would follow. And this time Styletto would be the headliner—other bands would open for *them.* "Eli," he had said, "I won't be back in L.A. until at least Christmas. I hope you're okay there.

"I'm sorry things have changed," Rick had said to Eli.

Change. There it was. Everything was changing all the time, Eli supposed, but it seemed like sometimes things changed faster than ever. After he talked to Rick he went into the bathroom and looked at himself in the mirror for a long time. The late afternoon sunlight streamed in through the window so that half of Eli's face was in deep shadow and the other half was bathed in golden sunlight. If he pulled his hair back on the shadowed side and tucked it into his shirt collar, he could imagine that one side of him was the old Eli he had already been and the other side was the new Eli, the person he was trying to become. He studied both reflections of himself carefully, then went to find Maud.

Eli had to do some fancy talking to convince Maud that he really wanted her to cut off his hair—he even had to resort to telling her about Amy. She did it, though. She got out her sewing shears and trimmed Eli's hair to the base of his neck. His long platinum hair that hadn't been cut for four years. His trademark.

Snip, snip, snip.

Two days before he was to appear before Judge Widmore, Eli went with Danny to a hair stylist in Eugene and had what was left of his hair cut to within an inch of his scalp. What Eli said when the woman asked what he wanted done was, "Just give me the hippest haircut in the universe, that's all," and that was what he got: short and spiky. If you're going to do something, he told everybody, you might as well do it right. Maud said he looked like his mother. He wondered what Rick would think.

The next Tuesday morning Eli did not go to school. Instead he rode with Danny and Maud into Salem so that he could testify before the judge about saving the trees. Diane Gooden met them in the lobby of the courthouse. She was surprised at the change in Eli's appearance. She told him he looked much older: "Like you're in high school," she said. The ceiling of the lobby was very high and their voices echoed from it. Eli noticed that everyone spoke quietly and walked quickly.

Diane—she would not let him call her Mrs. Gooden—quickly reminded Eli about the procedure. There would be a number of people testifying, she said, both for and against the clear-cut. The judge would call them in any order that suited him. Eli might be first or he might have to wait for hours. Diane reminded Eli to speak up when it was his turn, to be himself, to be positive, to smile. She explained to Danny and Maud what she and Eli had decided a few days ago on the phone: Eli would not read from a written statement, he would simply tell his story in his own words, make it up as he went along. Danny, who was far more nervous than Eli, was impressed by this. He put his arm around Eli's shoulders, gave the thumbs-up sign he always gave, and grinned. Eli could have more impact on the judge, Diane went on, if his personality could come across, if he could appear comfortable and sincere. She told them that she expected Judge Widmore to ask Eli some questions because of his youth and because of the fact that he was the "world-famous tree sitter." If Eli forgot to say anything important, it would come out when the judge questioned him. Diane asked him if he was ready. She and Maud both gave him a friendly hug, and the four of them entered the courtroom, Danny leading the way.

The room was large and carpeted, with upholstered seats rising in semicircular rows away from the bench. Acoustic paneling on the ceiling and walls absorbed sound. The hushed nature of the chamber and the people talking very quietly in small groups reminded Eli of one of those small movie theaters in shopping malls. He noticed Frank and some of his buddies sitting way in the back. Eli barely had time to get seated and look around before a man came in and said sternly, "All rise!" The judge walked in, and the hearing began.

All of the people who were in favor of cutting the trees testified first; Eli didn't get to talk until after two o'clock. When he did testify, it was exactly as Diane Gooden had told him it would be. He walked to the microphone and stated who he was and where he lived.

He could see the reels of a tape recorder turning lazily on a table in front of him. The judge listened intently with his head cocked to one side as Eli explained how he had been sent to live with Danny and Maud for the summer and how he had come to be involved with the big trees up the road from their farm. When he was telling about nearly being drowned in the river, some of Frank's group laughed and made jokes among themselves. The judge banged his gavel and told them sternly to be quiet or, he said, they would be asked to leave. Eli resisted the temptation to turn around and smirk at them. The judge asked Eli a few questions. Eli tried his best to answer them.

In the end, Judge Widmore ruled that the restraining order would remain in effect until June. At that time, he explained, another hearing would be held. Scientific evidence would be presented, including information about the importance of the watershed to the Moffett area and the number of northern spotted owls nesting in the vicinity. The judge explained briefly that the spotted owl was now officially a threatened species and that finding one or more nesting pairs could help determine whether or not the trees would be cut.

Eli was elated. He was hardly out of the courthouse and onto the sidewalk before he began to hug everyone at once—even Danny. In his excitement the words tumbled out, tripping over each other. He seemed barely able to keep his feet on the ground. Maud and Danny looked at each other, then at Eli, then back at one another and simply smiled, saying nothing, making Eli's joy their own. Diane Gooden, however, waited for Eli to calm down a bit, then put both hands on his shoulders and warned, "It's not over yet, Eli." She looked directly into his eyes, wanting his full attention. "They'll find lots of scientific evidence that says it's all right to cut those trees, that it won't hurt the watershed. Simpson will hire biologists who will say that no spotted owls nest anywhere near his trees. They'll make a good case. This could go on for years."

Eli shrugged, secure in his victory.

"It's very, very possible that after all is said and done we will lose, Eli. I just want you to know that." Then the lawyer brightened, took her hands from Eli's shoulders, and picked up her briefcase. "But, hey, we sure showed them today, didn't we?"

"Yeah," Eli agreed, remembering the summer and the grove of dark, silent trees. "We sure showed them today."

The Journey

Leave the crowded city
You got nothing to do
Ain't it just a pity
They're just picking on you

Born in California
Now you're leaving it behind
Head out to the country
You know it's so unkind

Whatcha gonna do there
When you're all alone
How you gonna handle
Being all alone

(Refrain)
Leave the crowded city
You got nothing to do
Ain't it just a pity
They're just picking on you

Pack up all your stuff
And you'll be on your way
There ain't no use to argue
There ain't nothing to say

(Refrain)

Small Town Blues

The end of a long journey
Is really just the start
When you get through with all your traveling
You'll find you ain't so smart

(Refrain)
I got them small town blues
I really can't believe that I'm here
How I came to this place
It sure ain't exactly clear

There are some that try to help you
And some that put you down
But those people never let you forget
You just got into town

(Refrain)

In the bright lights of the city
Nearly everyone is cool
But here the first man I run into
Is a redneck and a fool

(Refrain)

Narrow Minds

People call you names
People never care
People never see beyond
The way you cut your hair

Living in a crazy world
They hide behind the smile
Who can find the real you?
It's enough to drive you wild

They don't know where you're going
They don't know where you've been
But if you're just a little different
They act like it's a sin

Never mind what's in your heart
Forget what you've been taught
If you don't look and act like all the rest
You're likely to be shot

You can climb to the mountain
You can crawl like a snake
You can build a bridge to heaven
With all the dreams they'll break

Living in a crazy world
They hide behind the smile
Who can find the real you?
It's enough to drive you wild

Green River Death

Swirling, swirling
Falling away
The green river death
Almost got you today

The sky rushing past you
A wind in your ears
What only takes four seconds
Feels like twenty years

(Refrain)
Swirling, swirling
Falling away
The green river death
Almost got you today

The silence of the water
Is like the darkest night
Hey! What are those? Sharks?
Dark shapes just out of sight

(Refrain)

You try to make the surface
You can see it right up there
The sharks, they want to hold you
Want to keep you from the air

129

(Refrain)

You can soar like an eagle
But you'll drop like a stone
When it's the green river death
You'll have to go it alone

(Refrain)

Running

When it gets real bad
You're gonna fall, fall, fall
They say the story's sad
And that is all, all, all

Running for the trees
So you can hide, hide, hide
You gotta find your soul
And put it back inside

Yes, the story is the same one
Every place you go, go, go
It's got the same old ending
That you know, know, know

So you're running on the outside
Full of pain, pain, pain
Sprinting down the highway
So you won't go insane . . .

In the Peaceful Times

You find out who you are
In the peaceful times
You find out where you are
In the peaceful times

You get to know your friends
In the peaceful times
The circle of your life grows
In the peaceful times

You know where you're going
In the peaceful times
You know where you've been
In the peaceful times

Your life will sound like music
In the peaceful times
Your heart will be so light
In the peaceful times

The circle of your life grows
In the peaceful times
The circle of your life grows
In the peaceful times

A Secret Place

Listen and I'll tell you
About a secret place
Somewhere you can go
To escape the human race

It sings and it whispers
And it calls your name
It's hidden from the world
And it's always the same

It's dark and it's strange
It's full of mystery
Yet it sparkles like a diamond
Only you can see

Now they want to take it
Haul it all away
Turn it into gold
If they can find a way

Take It Into Your Own Hands

Turn to the left
They won't go
Turn to the right
They don't know
What can you do
When it's all up to you?

(Refrain)
Take it into your own hands
Yeah
Take it into your own hands
Just take it
Into your own hands

Sometimes people help you
Sometimes they don't
Sometimes they will
Sometimes they won't
What can you do
When it's all up to you?

(Refrain)

A little bit of action
Goes a long, long ways
It takes a little doing
But sometimes it pays
Whatcha gonna do
When it's all up to you?

(Refrain)

Bird

Like a bird
You sit in a tree
The days go by
You're wild and free

The sky above
The earth below
You can stay here if you like
But you're free to go

The moon and the sun
Are your only friends
You're part of this tree
As it creaks and bends

You would live here forever
If there was a way
If you could fly
You'd just sail away

Back on Earth

The people come to see you fall
They only point and stare
They giggle and they whisper
So you know that they don't care

They laugh at you, they call you names
They shake their heads in shame
They read it in the paper
You gave their town a bad name!

It's like you're on display
For all the folks to see
"Step right up, boys and girls
To see the weirdo in the tree."

When the right one comes, the one you trust
You'll know it right away
Her words are music in your ears
You'll be back on earth today